Echoes of Nobility

From the Echoes of History

By Lance Conrad

DAWN STAR
P R E S S

Echoes of Nobility

For information about discounts, bulk purchases, or reproduction of content in this book, please contact Dawn Star Press:

info@dawnstarpress.com

ISBN: 978-1-7333406-2-5

Printed in the United States of America

Dedicated to my brother, John.
You are a gifted writer and a
force for good in this tired world.

Chapter 1

Asher knelt before King Stephan.

Both king and fighter felt the absurdity of the gesture. Asher meant no fealty or deference by the action, and Stephan expected none.

It was as if the warrior was playing at subservience, like a father at a daughter's tea party.

Still, the fighter did it in style, sweeping his impressive cloak out to one side before dropping to one knee, his long, glossy hair falling about his face as he bowed low. The flair also served to show off the sword strapped to Asher's waist.

"However may I be of service, your magnificence?" Asher asked, bowing his face even lower to the ground.

King Stephan didn't laugh at the sarcasm. No one did. There was no one else in the throne room.

Moments like this didn't call for witnesses.

"Asher, son of Parthan, called the Laughing Killer by his own men. Thank you for coming."

"My king," Asher started, a twitch of a smile on his lips. "You'll forgive me, but I always preferred the Marauders' title for me."

"Gholost? Hunger? It is a dark thing, man."

"Still, it makes me smile." Asher matched the words with the expression, a devilish grin spreading across his face. "So, my king, again I ask, what can I do for you?"

"You can answer for your actions during the war," the king replied.

Asher lifted his head to dramatically raise an eyebrow.

"My actions, noble sire? To what actions do you refer? Am I here to receive some award for ending the war early? Nearly half of their greatest captains died at my hand."

"We both know that's not all you did, Asher."

Asher sneered and rose the rest of the way to his feet.

"Is this about General Rathbar? The fool should thank me. With only one hand, it looks like he actually did something in the war."

"You know full well that Rathbar was and is one of my most competent commanders. If it hadn't been your own wife in the camp, I doubt you would have cared or even noticed."

"The fact remains that it was my wife." Asher's light tone turned a little darker.

"The fact remains that you attacked a superior officer and deserted!" King Stephan shot back.

"I'd hardly call Rathbar superior." Asher drawled, but he was already making a show of searching the

2

corners of the room, turning his head dramatically one way, then the other.

"There seems to be a few pieces missing, my liege, if you truly mean to hold me accountable. At first, I'd been looking forward to seeing one of your famous trials. I hear you demand witnesses and everything. Sounds like quite a show.

"I don't see any such people here. In fact, this looks a lot more like the old ways, when a chief's anger was reason enough for a death sentence.

"However, if it was your intention to simply make me disappear, then there's another thing I'm not seeing: a lot more men. Do you intend to do the job yourself? I'd respect that. You would die trying, but I'd respect you for it."

Stephan ignored the comments and started on his own, casual observations

"It's been a couple years since the end of the war. How is life treating you? Are you keeping busy?"

"A farmer is always busy." Asher responded simply, rising to his feet, growing tired of the show of kneeling.

"You dress rather nicely for a farmer." Stephan noted. It was true, Asher's boots were polished black leather. His shirt was white silk. The cloak he swirled around him was velvety black, with purple trim on the inside. "Do you enjoy a farmer's life?"

"There's nothing to enjoy or not enjoy. It's just a life. I have always been a farmer. For a time, I was a farmer who killed a lot of Marauders. What's your point? Yes, it's been a while, I thought maybe you had decided to leave well enough alone."

"Justice can never be left alone, Asher. An answer must be given."

"Then you really do intend to kill me." Asher grinned his first true smile of the night, as if he were delighted by the idea. "Do you have men hidden in the halls, then? They must be very fast indeed if you expect them to make it to me before I make it to you. Shall I get the ball rolling?"

Asher took a menacing step forward, but Stephan didn't flinch. He waved his hand as if shooing away a fly.

"None of that. Don't get me wrong, many of my advisers have suggested such a thing. Most agree that you are too dangerous to be left alive."

"But you don't agree?"

"I might, but I've always believed that the side of good needs dangerous men as well. I already know that you are a dangerous man. Are you a good man, Asher?"

Asher scoffed.

"What are you trying to get at here? I don't believe you are a fool, and there is no chance you haven't read the reports. Do you think I'm a good man, Stephan?"

The king took a moment and considered the question, then shook his head.

"Probably not," he admitted. "Still, I don't think you're like the Marauders, or some other men I know, who aren't as straightforward as you are. You see, Asher, these last couple years haven't been idle. I've been keeping an eye on you."

"Yes, I see your men lurking in the shadows." Asher nodded. "What did you hope to learn from that? How I plow my fields? How I like my potatoes?"

"Having my guards keep an eye out for you in the marketplace is hardly 'lurking in shadows,'" Stephan said wryly. "But it's funny you should mention potatoes. You don't buy potatoes in the market, do you? You buy turnips."

The king smiled with an odd enthusiasm. "It took some time, but we managed to put something together. You don't like turnips. We have questioned all of your men, and everyone we could find who knew you as a child. All confirm that you'll go hungry before you eat a turnip."

Asher's mouth opened, but he found no words for several seconds.

"Turnips? You questioned my friends about turnips? What are you on about?"

"You buy turnips every week, without fail," Stephan interrupted.

"Well, yes, they don't grow well on my farm. But they're not for me, they're for..." Asher's face fell and he took a step back. It wasn't a retreat, however, Asher had slipped into a fighting stance. A snarl curled his lip.

"Eliana." Stephan finished for him. "You buy them for Eliana. She loves turnips. We even have reports of you, Asher, eating turnips in her presence."

"Are you threatening her, Stephan?" Asher's back curled and his feet shifted, moving his weight forward, ready to pounce. For the first time, Stephan looked worried.

"No, Asher, no, I am not threatening Eliana in any way. I only bring it up because I know that you care about her."

"So?" Asher demanded, now completely in his battle stance. One hand hovered near his sword, the other behind his back where a dagger waited. Without leaving his seat on the throne, Stephan had pushed Asher off balance.

"So you have at least that much goodness in you," Stephan said. "A man in love with a good woman will never be a true villain, not completely. It is that nugget of goodness that I need from you."

"Why would I do anything for you?" Asher growled. "I don't owe you anything. I did more to end the war than any other soldier. My conscience is clear."

"Your conscience? Now, let's not get crazy. I've read the reports and you lived them. Pillage? Executing prisoners? Torture? I think we can both agree you don't have anything like a conscience. You are going to help me because I have something you want, and you have something I want. What I offer here is a trade."

"You don't have anything I want." Asher shot back. "If you did, I would take it from you."

"My silence." Stephan commented calmly. "You want my silence. Those reports and everything in them are under my control. We have not released any part of them to the people. There are rumors, of course, but Eliana doesn't listen to rumors, does she? Not that she'd get a chance, since you are always the one to go to the market. Why is that, Asher? Are you afraid she might hear something about your efforts in the war?"

Asher took a step forward.

"Asher," Stephan warned. "There are multiple copies of a letter left with my advisers. If I die tonight, your war record and the news of my death at your hand will be published across the kingdom."

Asher stopped.

"What do you want from me?" Asher's tone made Stephan shiver. He had planned everything so well, he thought, but now he knew the distinct fear of someone who has wounded a wild animal.

"I need you to kill some people."

Asher relaxed, a new grin spreading across his face.

"You should have opened with that, my king. I'm a simple man. I appreciate simple discussion. Who is it you want killed... and how?"

Asher licked at his lips and Stephan shivered again.

"That is part of the issue. I don't know any names, not for certain."

"Tsk, tsk, my king," Asher scolded, back in his comfort zone. "If I am to be your royal assassin, I will require better information. Or shall I start with those disloyal to you and work outward?"

"It's not like that!" Stephan snapped. "There's not going to be any 'royal assassin.' I'm not going to be that kind of king. These people fought, bled, and died for me. They and their families deserve rule of law, consistency, and protection. I'm going to give that to them."

"A nice speech, Stephan. And yet, here I am... and here you are."

Stephan grated his teeth, but there was no argument he could offer.

"This is a one-time thing." he insisted, ignoring Asher's scoff at the idea. "There is a group of criminals, the Tribulus, who have organized with the express purpose of circumventing the law. They know of my necessity for witnesses. So, they come and testify for each other, or make other witnesses against them disappear. Now I hear rumors of them starting to take children, as a warranty for people's silence."

"So much for rule of law." Asher sneered.

"No!" Stephan shouted back, louder than he

should have, he knew. He continued in a more controlled tone. "The people can handle it. I believe in our people. It is only this one group that manipulates the system. I'm not going to discard justice and return to tyranny for one group of thieves and murderers. I just... I just need them to go away."

The last sentence was said fervently and through clenched teeth. Asher smiled at that. He knew what it had taken from the king to admit this. It was admitting the flaw in his system.

Rule of law only worked with a population that was generally trying to be good. When you had a group like this one who shamelessly pursued evil, there was a lot of damage they could do before the law could catch up to them.

"I think I can help you, for the right price." Asher was more relaxed now. As Stephan had leverage on him, he now had leverage on the king.

"Your price is clemency!" King Stephan shot back. "I know you don't want Eliana knowing about that village by the river, for example."

Asher grinned back, unashamed.

"You're right, of course. I don't want her to know about that. Probably in the same way you wouldn't want people to know about this conversation. The king killing people in secret? I don't think you want that information getting out to the kingdom, or to your family, or your son."

Asher looked to the side meaningfully. Stephan

was drawing breath to yell back when he caught Asher's gesture. He leaned over to see what Asher was looking at.

A small boy, only a few years old, stood there by the throne dais. His nightshirt hung low to the ground and he dragged a small knit blanket behind him.

"Tibian!" Stephan snapped. The boy jumped. "What are you doing up? Get to bed this instant!"

Stephan started out of his throne, as if to come after the boy, but it wasn't necessary. The child ran, as only small children can, tripping once over his nightshirt, then scrambling up to keep running.

Stephan looked back to Asher, who was still grinning wolfishly at the whole domestic display.

"A little hard on the boy, weren't you?" Asher drawled, enjoying the king's embarrassment. Surprisingly, Stephan nodded.

"You may be right. I'll make it up to him tomorrow. He's my youngest, Tibian. He was born during the war and I'm still getting to know him. He's a tough one in most things, but he always cries when I yell."

Asher blinked. He had been in the middle of a negotiation, a battle of sorts. He'd already had his next five arguments ready to launch. The king's sudden honesty and vulnerability left him feeling off-balance.

"I wouldn't know. I don't have any kids," Asher said, quieter now.

"Not yet, anyway." Stephan smiled now. "Do you

think my watchers would have missed that Eliana is pregnant?"

Asher smiled and nodded. Like two gears clicking together, king and killer were suddenly just two men, fathers, who understood each other. The moment didn't last long, but it left a deep mark.

"So, what is your price, then?" Stephan asked, not as a challenge, but as an offer.

"I ask for the opposite of your threat," Asher said. "I understand this job can't be made known to the people, but if I pull it off, I want you to make it known that I was a great help in the war, a hero."

"I can do that." Stephan shrugged, surprised at the low price. "Of course, you know, those who were close to the situation will know that's a lie."

"Those close to the situation know how to keep their mouths shut," Asher growled, serious again. "You're the king. The common people, the ones who drool stories around the market, will believe you."

And Eliana. The words went unsaid, but were heard all the same. *Eliana will believe.*

"I trust you understand that if you breathe a word about this to anyone, the deal is off," King Stephan noted.

"Of course, my king, not a word," Asher lied. Of course, he would bring in some help on a job this big. But he knew he could trust his men. Nothing would get back to Stephan on his throne.

"Then we have a deal." Stephan agreed readily.

The price was low enough, and only served as confirmation that there was something still human in this man.

All of his humanity might center around a single person, but that was enough for some people. Besides, Stephan wasn't sure he had a choice. The Tribulus was getting more brazen. The last time he had convinced a group of business owners to come out against them, two shops were burned down, one man was killed, and everyone else suddenly became quite forgetful.

The people were scared. They looked to their king for protection, but guards could only be spread so thin before they became targets themselves. In any gap, the Tribulus could strike and melt away before anyone could respond.

They were nightmares. And how did one fight a nightmare? Stephan looked at the retreating back of Asher and knew the answer.

You sent a demon.

Chapter 2

Asher entered the night and breathed in the darkness. He had always felt comfortable in the dark, even as a child. Light had always meant hard toil under a hot sun, back when he was a farmer's son. Light meant people watching you, trying to guess what you were thinking behind your silence.

Darkness, on the other hand, was cool, quiet, and solitary. It felt right.

The feeling gave him a little extra spring in his step as he wandered away from the castle. He didn't head home, not yet. Eliana was a heavy sleeper and hadn't noticed him leave. She wouldn't be up before the sun, which gave Asher a few more hours to return to his house and sneak back into bed.

Stephan had offered to give what details he knew about the organization he was hunting, but Asher had waved him off. He felt like it would ruin it somehow, knowing too much at the start.

There was a little voice in the back of his head suggesting to him that this might be his last chance. He couldn't quite voice what it was he was losing, but he felt it slipping away all the same. Every day that he put in an honest day's work, he felt something within him grow more dull. Every time he talked to another villager with a dumb, round, honest face, he felt like a rusting blade.

His hand traced the handle of his sword. He wore it everywhere, but hadn't drawn it in months, not even to sharpen it. This was the blade everyone looked at, however, which was useful. He'd won many battles because people were watching his right hand on the hilt of his sword. Few had enough awareness to even flinch when Asher's left hand whipped forward with a thrown dagger.

He always aimed for the face. Even if he missed, people would overreact trying to protect their face. Before they had regained their balance, Asher would close the distance and the sword they'd been watching so closely would slide in.

Asher sighed.

That was what he was losing. The land had united, won the war, and become a kingdom in the process. Asher had also won, in his own way. He had felt more free than any other time in his life during the war. He had won every battle in which he had fought and returned home to the adoring eyes of his wife.

He had won.

And now he had needed to clean rust from his daggers when he had pulled them out of their box earlier today. What would happen now?

King Stephan was strengthening the Land Guard day by day. Their borders were becoming stronger and safer. More and more, to Asher, they were starting to feel like walls.

He would farm. Eliana would be happy. He'd help her raise their children. But what would happen to his blades? They would grow old and dull. They would rust or become farm tools. In his mind, he had already accepted this. Life moved on, didn't it?

But in his heart, he thrilled at this new assignment from the king. He could be Hunger again, even if this might be the last time.

The same little voice in his head prayed that it would not end quickly, or peacefully.

"So?" The voice came out of the darkness, so close the speaker could have put a hand on Asher's shoulder. It was always like this. Every interaction with Baba started as an ambush. Asher suspected she enjoyed watching people jump.

Asher didn't jump.

He had been expecting her. He always expected her whenever it seemed like he was alone. While it made him a little jumpy whenever he had to go to the bathroom, he was generally grateful for the paranoia she instilled. It kept him sharp.

"You vile old hag!" he snapped, though both of them knew there was no real venom behind it. "What gives you the right to sneak around and scare innocent people?"

"Have you seen any innocent people out at this time of night?" she shot back, looking dramatically from side to side, as if some pink-cheeked child might suddenly appear from the shadows. "I only saw one, and the youth was scurrying back to warm blankets after visiting the privy."

"I hope the poor child didn't see you. You would give the thing nightmares for the rest of its life."

"You know, if you're going to have a brat of your own, it would help if you started thinking of a child as something other than an 'it.'"

Asher grinned and shrugged his shoulders. She was right, of course, Baba usually was. That was one of the most unnerving things about her. Someone that crazy shouldn't be right that often.

"So?" She repeated her query in her reedy, old-hag voice. Asher didn't actually know how old she was. No one did. By all appearances, she was ancient, nearly on the edge of death. That didn't mean anything with Baba, though. She could very well be younger than he was. While Asher guarded his own secrets zealously, he knew he had nothing on the Trash Lady. Every single thing about her seemed to be a lie or a cover.

She lived in the streets, often sleeping in trash piles, or worse, though Asher knew where she kept some things, including a decent amount of money. The smell coming off of her kept everyone at least five paces away at all times. If the smell didn't work, she was known to talk to herself, screaming at random, scaring nearby people.

Asher had once offered to get her a place to stay and clean up. She had only smiled at him, patted his cheek with a hand nearly black from grime and said, "Nobody looks at trash," as if that explained everything.

"I've been given a job by our king," he stated simply. "I'll be going to get a couple of men to help. Could you start looking around?"

"I never stop looking around," she scoffed. "Tell me exactly what it is you need, and I'll decide what part I want to play."

Asher nodded. Baba had a strange fascination with him, so she would listen to him, but nobody commanded her.

"I'm going to be taking on the Tribulus."

Asher smiled inwardly at already flouting his deal with the king by telling Baba. She wasn't a danger, he knew. She kept secrets obsessively. Besides, giving her information was the best way to get some in return.

Baba's eyes widened slightly at the name and she gave a low whistle of appreciation.

"A tough bit of meat, to be sure. Shall I find one of their number? A thread you can pull on?"

Asher shook his head.

"The Tribulus are sure to hear about it if someone is looking for them."

Baba nodded with a small smile, as if Asher had passed some little test.

"Instead, find me a victim. I need somebody who is being extorted by the Tribulus, but someone without a family."

"A clever move," Baba nodded. "The Tribulus is known for finding leverage. Have you given any thought to your own family?"

Asher stopped walking. As always, the thought of Eliana in danger stoked a primal rage deep inside.

"They would dare come after her?" he asked.

"They are a daring organization. And they know how to find weak spots. Yours is your wife."

Asher ground his teeth together. She was right. So then, a new problem, where to leave her?

He turned to ask Baba another question about the Tribulus and their reach, but she was already gone.

Asher strained to hear her footsteps, knowing he wouldn't. He could never figure out how she moved so quietly. If nothing else, her rags should shuffle and whisper as she moved. Maybe they were too dirty to rustle, he mused.

Then Baba was out of his mind and he walked swiftly through the darkness. His feet found the paths on their own, leaving his mind to wander and scheme.

He had to assume the worst. It was the only safe way to operate. Therefore, he assumed that the Tribulus would be able to gather information on him, his old men, and his common spots.

So, it had to be somewhere he had never been, someone he wasn't connected to, but still someone he could trust with the safety of his wife.

It was a twisting puzzle.

He nearly bumped into his cabin before he realized he was home. He leaned against the sturdy wooden wall of his cabin and thought it through.

They wouldn't be able to tie him to Baba. Baba never let herself be publicly connected to anyone. But that didn't do him much good. He couldn't send Eliana to stay with Baba. There weren't enough words in the world to explain why he wanted his wife to go live with a beggar for a few days.

Who were Eliana's friends? He wished now that he had paid more attention when she talked about them. She didn't see them much anymore, anyway. She had slowly been pulled into his isolated way of living, especially since her father had died. She didn't have any other family.

Then, suddenly, he had it. Asher smiled in the darkness.

"The do-gooder," he whispered.

Chapter 3

"And of course, my Asher was the only one they trusted to do it," Eliana bragged to Ander and his wife, Rachel. They both smiled and nodded.

Eliana always bragged about Asher.

"So, guard work, eh?" Ander smiled. "That will be a nice change of pace for you."

"That's true," Asher confirmed. "I fear my back will break if I have to bend over and pick up one more rock. Still, with Eliana this close to her time, I worry about her at that house all alone. Again, thank you."

"Don't even mention it!" Rachel gushed. "It'll be nice to have someone around to help watch the boys. They're such rascals."

Asher looked to the two boys she was referring to. The younger one was playing quietly in the yard, throwing rocks at a stick. Young children could be amused by the simplest things. The older one, who was maybe ten years old, sat next to his father.

Asher found that one particularly unnerving. What was his name again? Asher hadn't really paid attention during the introduction. Something starting with an "M" perhaps, or maybe an "S?" It was probably just as well Asher didn't know the boy's name, or he might have snapped at him by now.

The boy's eyes had been trained on Asher from the first moment he stepped in, studying him. It was unnerving how it seemed like the boy was looking right through him. Worst of all, the boy's head would tilt ever so slightly to the left whenever Asher lied, as if he knew, every single time. He had faced men with swords who were less intimidating than this small child with his creepy silence and piercing gaze.

Asher smiled and chatted his way through the simple meal, doing his best to avoid looking at the older son, who continued to watch him. Finally, chairs were pushed back and Rachel pulled Eliana away to get a bed set up for her.

Ander nodded his head towards the door and walked out. Asher followed.

Neither Asher or Ander were smoking men, so there wasn't much pretense for heading out into a moonless night like this one without any kind of light. Even Asher, who had exceptional night vision, couldn't see more than a few yards in front of him by the dim starlight.

"I don't expect you to tell me what you're really up to, Asher," Ander began.

"I told you the truth," Asher asserted. "There's a caravan that needs an extra couple of guards. This is my first time with them, so I don't know how long I'll be gone."

"The truth? Asher, you'd lie if the truth sounded better," Ander scolded. "Fact is that guard work pays better than farming these days. So much better, in fact, that I've been down in the city every single day checking for jobs. The last caravan left a week ago and the next one won't be ready for weeks yet."

"Maybe you missed one," Asher grunted.

"Not a chance. I have been checking with the tallow merchants. No caravan leaves town without a substantial purchase of grease for the wheels. So those particular merchants always know the caravans, even those who try to keep their travels secret."

"Clever," Asher remarked. He meant it. Tracking supplies rather than men was smart. Supplies were harder to hide than men.

"It was Simeon's idea, actually."

"Who?"

"My son, the one who's been staring at you all night."

Ah, Simeon. That was it. This new information did nothing to make Asher like him any more. A kid that age shouldn't be that clever. It was weird.

"Right, that Simeon," Asher shrugged.

"The point is, you're lying about where you're going. Then, you brought your wife here. It's not that I'm not grateful for you saving my life during the war, but we haven't really spoken since then. Why bring your wife here?"

Asher didn't answer. Maybe he should have pondered this a little more. He had come to Ander because he knew he was trustworthy, almost to a fault. He hadn't really expected clever. Clever got people into trouble. Ander doubled down by answering his own question.

"You brought her here because you're about to do something dangerous," Ander mused. "But no, that's not enough. If it were simply a matter of you dying, you'd have your men see to it that she was looked after. You're going to do something that might have repercussions, people coming after her, perhaps? You brought her here because nobody would connect you and me. Is that it?"

Asher fumed in the darkness. Why couldn't he have been some big, noble clod with a sharp sword and dull wit?

"I won't endanger your family, if that's what you're worried about."

"That's exactly what I'm worried about," Ander confirmed. "This has got to be something local, right? You wouldn't worry about Marauders knowing where your wife lives. And it's got to be a group, since if it were just a couple of people, they'd be dead before they could even ask who was attacking them. I'm guessing you're going after the Tribulus, right?"

"You need to keep your mouth shut," Asher hissed. "You're as creepy as your boy in there. I asked you to give my wife a place to sleep for a few days. What do you want? Gold? Don't you try to blackmail me, farmer."

"Settle down." Ander's voice was entirely too calm. Asher was beginning to regret coming to this family with their big smiles and sharp eyes. "Your wife will be safe here. Our land will be better with those vermin gone. Still, you owe me for this. And no, I don't want gold."

"What do you want, then?"

"Peace of mind."

Asher laughed at that.

"You have gravely misunderstood my skill set, farmer. Peace of mind isn't really what I bring to the table."

"Last week, during a storm, a tree branch cracked in the wind and fell right in front of me. It could have killed me."

"We all die," Asher quipped. "You're not going to convince me you're a coward now."

"No, I'm not a coward. I am mortal, though. And if something happens to me and Rachel, I want you to look after my boys."

"Again, farmer, you misunderstand my skill set. I'm no babysitter, either."

"I'm not looking for that," Ander assured him. "I want a thumb on the scales. If they're in danger, I want them out. Is that clear enough?"

"Fine," Asher agreed. This was starting to feel more comfortable. He could picture it now. The creepy boy would grow up thinking he was smarter than everybody and annoy some dangerous people, maybe run up some gambling debts. Smart people always got themselves in trouble gambling. The dangerous people would try to have the creepy boy injured or killed as an example, then Asher would kill the dangerous people instead. Not a bad way to spend a weekend and Asher's world made sense again.

The two men shook on it in the darkness.

"Then let's get back inside. I imagine you'll want to say goodnight to your wife before you get to work."

Chapter 4

Asher knocked on Mendar's front door first thing the following morning. While waiting for someone to answer, Asher admired the handiwork. He had known, on some level, that Mendar enjoyed working with wood, but he'd never seen any examples of his lieutenant's work. This was the first time he'd come to visit.

"Asher?" Mendar opened the door with a jerk, the question already on his lips. Asher smiled. Of course, Mendar already knew who was at the door before he opened it. Most soldiers made it through the war by luck alone. Mendar survived because he was careful.

"What's wrong?" Mendar asked, scanning Asher quickly for any wounds.

"Nothing is wrong," Asher comforted him. "At least, not for us. But I need your help causing a little trouble for some others."

"Come inside." Mendar opened the door wider to admit Asher, doing a quick sweep of the field beyond the door. It was no mistake that there was a wide open space in front of the house.

"You remember Sarah." Mendar waved towards

his wife who was bouncing an infant on her hip. She gave Asher a cold look. This puzzled Asher, as he barely remembered the woman. They certainly hadn't spent enough time together for him to have caused her some offense.

"Of course! How lovely to see you again." Asher bowed, sweeping out his fine cloak to one side as he bent his knee in a showy bow. Women always liked that sort of thing.

Sarah rolled her eyes, sent a scowl towards her husband, and left the room.

"Everything all right at home, Mendar?" Asher asked, his eyebrow raised.

"Oh yes, everything is fine. She's just afraid you're here to drag me back to a life of violence." He sank into a chair. He waved Asher into the chair facing his before getting back to business. "Asher, are you here to drag me back to a life of violence?"

"Just one job." Asher shrugged. "I'll make sure you get paid well for your efforts."

"It's not worth it." Mendar waved his hand, as if physically dismissing the idea. "I have regular commissions now. I make plenty of money as a builder and I don't have to kill anyone."

"You're sure I can't change your mind?" Asher asked.

"Quite certain," Mendar nodded.

"Then I guess I'll take on the Tribulus on my own." Asher stood and moved towards the door.

"The Tribulus?" Mendar was on his feet as well. "Asher, I'd advise you to stay far away from all of that. If half of what I've heard is true, that group is serious trouble. Have you heard that they've started taking children?"

"Baba mentioned something like that."

Mendar's nose crinkled.

"The Trash Lady? I don't know how you can even stand close enough to her to have a conversation."

Asher shrugged. "She's interesting. It also helps that I can't actually smell much. Long story, but a badly broken nose didn't heal right on the inside."

"The point is," Mendar continued, leaning forward and rubbing his temples. "Is that anyone who angers these people isn't just endangering themselves, they also put everyone they know on the chopping block. The Tribulus excels at finding leverage."

"I've got Eliana hidden away until this is done."

"That's fine for you, but I don't have anywhere I can hide my wife and children. She wouldn't go, anyway. I love her, but she might be more stubborn than you."

"Like I said, I'll do it without you," Asher remarked, opening the door.

"That hardly matters!" Mendar slammed the door closed, nearly catching Asher's fingers. "Unless you manage to decapitate this thing quickly, they'll figure out it's you attacking them. Then they'll not only go after your wife, but everyone associated with you,

28

which includes me and mine!"

"So it does," Asher deadpanned. "What's your way out, then?"

Mendar ran his hand through his hair, gripping it at the end, breathing heavily.

"You're not going to call this off, are you?" He didn't look at Asher as he asked it.

"I'm surprised you'd even ask. When have we ever done a job half-way? Besides, you were always the one with the soft spot. Are you really going to ask me to leave them alone to save your family while they steal other people's children?"

"Would you have me believe you're doing this for the greater good?" Mendar snapped.

"No, I'm actually doing it for Stephan."

This brought Mendar up short.

"The King? How did he convince you to get involved?"

"He asked nicely and offered a price that interested me. Look, I can't claim a great deal of civic responsibility, but even I can see that these Tribulus people are only getting stronger. I certainly don't want to be looking over my shoulder when my child is out there in the world. If you're in danger anyway, what's your best option?"

Mendar drew a deep breath, then changed. It was a subtle thing, but Asher had been looking for it. He was one of the few who knew that Mendar was two people. One was the loving father and devoted craftsman. But Asher had seen Mendar backed into a corner by Marauders. He had seen him watch friends die, then stand to avenge them. Oh yes, there was another version of Mendar, and it looked out at him now and spoke the words Asher had been waiting to hear.

"Let's kill them all."

Chapter 5

The other person Asher wanted for the team was much easier to recruit.

"Tormand?" Mendar asked with a sneer. "Leave him to rot where he is. Asher, if we're doing this, then let's do it right. Give me half a day and I'll have the entire squad back together. We can face the Tribulus with two dozen proven killers of men."

Asher waved away the idea.

"We want to keep this small for as long as we can. If we make too much noise before we find out where they are and how many they are, we'll only be creating more targets for them. That would be a lot of families to try and protect."

Mendar thought this over and grudgingly agreed. It was a good reason not to involve the squad. It was even true, though Asher had to admit it wasn't his real reason.

He couldn't shake the feeling that this was his last job, one last rampage of blood before the long haul of a farmer's life ground him into the land he worked.

He had a vision in his mind of how he wanted this to go, and it didn't involve spending a lot of time around a planning table, giving orders to men who went out and exterminated the Tribulus. No, Asher fully intended to get his hands dirty. The more people who got involved, the harder that became.

They knew they were close to the slaughterhouse long before they saw it. Even Asher's limited sense of smell could pick up on the overwhelming miasma of livestock and death.

An operation like this was a natural consequence of city life. Farmers outside the city killed their own meat. A single cow or pig could take days of processing, curing, and/or drying, depending on what the family needed. Even the hide and bones were turned into something useful, nothing wasted.

In the city, things couldn't be done with such care and thoroughness. People had to be fed, so a lot of animals needed to die every day. That meant assembly lines, a machine of death.

No one stopped Asher and Mendar as they stepped into the building. This was not the sort of place that needed security. You had to pay people well to work in the slaughterhouse, everyone else with any sense kept well away, happy to buy their meat in neat paper packages, far from the sights, sounds, and smells that put meat in that paper.

They found Tormand quickly. He was at the front of the long line. He was the one who held the actual knife that killed the animals, then a heavy winch hoisted the carcass into the air to be taken to the next step of the process, usually skinning.

Asher waited until Tormand looked up from his work, wiping sweat from his brow with the back of a bloody hand. Then he locked eyes with Asher.

Asher beckoned.

Tormand dropped his long, thin knife to the ground, letting it clatter behind him as he stripped off his heavy apron.

A supervisor of some kind called after him, trying to get him to come back, but Tormand paid no mind. He smiled broadly, blood splatter on his face.

"Captain! Do you have a job for me? Please tell me you do. Killing cattle and pigs lacks... flavor."

"I'll wait outside," Mendar muttered in disgust and walked away. He knew all too well what kind of "flavor" Tormand enjoyed.

"Yes, I need information from the unwilling."

Tormand's bright smile would have been at home on a child seeing his first pony.

"I can start now!" he said. "Or do we need to catch them first?"

"We'll need to catch a few of them." Asher confirmed. "It might take a while."

"Is it the whole crew together?"

"Just you, me, Mendar, and Baba."

Tormand's face squinted in disgust.

"You sure know how to spoil a party. I don't know which smells worse, the Trash Lady or Mendar's self-righteous airs. You won't let them get in my way?"

"You answer to me. No one else. But make no mistake, you answer to me. If you go off plan, you're done."

"Good enough for me." Tormand chuckled, rubbing his bloody hands together. "Let's get started!"

Chapter 6

"Hey there!" Mendar and Tormand jumped as Baba spoke right behind them. Once again, Asher managed to maintain his air of calm. They hadn't specified a meeting place, so that meant that either Asher would need to find Baba, or she would need to find him. It stung, but Asher knew full well which would happen.

"You'd think I could smell you coming," Tormand griped, moving farther away from the woman as she breathed toward him, her breath nearly green with the smell of old garlic.

"She always approaches from downwind," Asher noted. "You should take a moment and wonder where she learned to do that. It is something for hunters, not beggars. Have you found someone for me?

The last question was said louder and was directed to Baba.

"This way." The Trash Lady turned and walked off, never looking back to see if they followed.

"Has she found the Tribulus?" Tormand asked. He loosened his sword in its sheath. "I didn't expect things to take off so quickly."

Mendar rolled his eyes.

"Of course not, you idiot!" he snapped. He had never been able to stand Tormand. Every word the man uttered seemed to set Mendar off. "All we have is rumors. We have no real idea how big the Tribulus is or who they have working for them. Until we get the lay of the land, we can't even let them know we're looking. I'm sure Asher has come up with some other way of looking for them. Please tell me you have."

Asher flashed a wide grin at Mendar, amused by the sliver of desperate hope in his tone.

"Naturally, I have. We're going after the victims. We also need a base of operations. Unless I miss my guess, Baba is leading us somewhere we can find both."

"Going after the victims?" Tormand asked with a smile. "What an incredible phrase. And you're sure we're the good guys in this?"

"We're the men who are going to get the job done. And don't pretend for a second you care how 'good' we are doing it."

"Fair point," Tormand admitted.

Asher crinkled his nose. Baba had led them down by the river, downstream of many of the businesses that dumped waste into the water. The smell felt like it was seeping into his skin. He shouldn't have worn his good cloak.

"There." Baba pointed a crooked finger at an inn,

36

one of the only ones in the area. "The innkeeper. His name is Vander. He inherited the land from his father. He had the brilliant idea of selling alcohol to the river workers, which worked well until better inns opened closer to the wharfs. He still does all right, though, in spite of appearances."

The appearances were shabby, indeed. Like many men with a good idea and little else, he had clearly skimped on most of his building costs. The boards hadn't been painted and now most peeled and warped, the gaps filled after the fact with mud and daub. Asher shook his head. If the river ever flooded, the whole place would wash away.

"Is this the best..." Asher started, turning towards Baba, but she was already gone.

Mendar shivered.

"Not exactly one for a hug goodbye, is she? Not that I'm sorry."

"She gave us what we needed. From here, it's on us. For starters, we need the innkeeper alone. Get rid of anyone else, but make it subtle."

They moved into the inn and fanned out. Asher went straight for the bar, where a portly fellow stood pouring a drink for a bearded man.

"Give me a moment, sir, I'll be right with you," the barkeeper said, his eyes roving over Asher's fine cloak with a hungry look.

"Oh, take your time. I'll be here all night," Asher said, never breaking eye contact. The intensity of the look and the odd comment froze Vander for a second and the drink overflowed, sloshing onto his hand. He swore and handed the overfull glass to the waiting patron, who glanced at Asher and moved quickly to a table.

There was no peace for him there, however. Mendar and Tormand were already hard at work. Mendar had chosen to be threatening, making a show of his sword and trying to start fights with the other patrons.

Tormand had gone the other way and was being overly friendly, giving hugs, asking names, and sipping from people's drinks, assuring them that he would buy the next round, or maybe the one after that.

While Mendar managed to bully a few into leaving, Tormand's technique was far superior. Men like this could drink through somebody throwing their weight around, but nobody liked a friendly mooch.

Vander saw his patrons starting to polish off their drinks and head for the door after a smiling Tormand threw an arm around their neck and suggested a song. He looked annoyed and started to move around the bar to intervene.

"Stay." Asher didn't even look up from where he was tracing lines on the bar with his finger and a stray drop of water.

"Did you say something, sir?" Vander paused. Asher looked up and met his eyes.

"I told you to stay behind your filthy bar. My friends are going to give us some privacy here shortly and we'll have ourselves a talk. But if I see you move your fat carcass before we're ready for you, we'll have our talk outside, warmed by the fire of your inn burning to the ground. Did you hear me alright that time?"

The man froze, nodding his understanding.

Asher glanced back as Mendar "accidentally" broke a man's little finger as they fought over a chair. The man cursed and yelled, but walked out of the inn. Only a couple customers remained, and Tormand had just kissed one on the cheek, while his free hand casually dipped two fingers in the other man's glass.

"Look, if this is a robbery," Vander started, but Asher turned and silenced him with a look.

"I told you to shut up and wait," he hissed. "Polish a glass or make a sandwich, whatever you people do."

Vander wisely chose to place both hands on the bar and wait patiently as the last two men took their leave. The door closed behind them and Mendar shoved the bolt home, locking the door after them.

All three men turned to Vander, who was now trembling, sweat rolling down his face as the two other men folded in behind him, trapping him, as if he had had anywhere to run.

"Perhaps you should sit down."

Mendar produced a length of rope and tied the

man's hands behind him, then guided him into a chair, which creaked under his weight.

Tormand looked hungry, and Asher had to admit that this would normally be his area of expertise, but Tormand tended to get carried away, and they would need this one functional and compliant for an indeterminate amount of time.

Chapter 7

Impressively, by the time they got him seated, the innkeeper had already calmed down. He eyed Asher up and down. Good, there was intelligence there. Asher liked the intelligent ones. There was something arrogant in their eyes as they tried to outsmart him. He loved watching them break.

Asher planted a foot firmly on the man's wide, soft chest and kicked. The chair under him had already been straining bravely under the load, but this was too much. The wood splintered as the bartender fell back. He whimpered and scrambled, with his hands still tied behind his back, trying to right himself from the wreckage of the chair.

"Should we get him another seat?" Mendar drawled.

"I don't care," Asher snapped. "This one doesn't matter."

The bartender, who had managed to get his knees under him, looked up in alarm.

"Did you still want to talk to him, or should we kill him, like the others?" Mendar asked. Asher took a moment to consider this, leaning his head back and forth, as if weighing the options. He enjoyed the little bit of theater from his men. He hadn't even prepared them beforehand. They had great instincts for this kind of thing.

Asher had taught and trained every one of them to fight, but more than that, he had taught them how to defeat an enemy, and that didn't always include sharp edges. Any man in Asher's crew knew how to attack the mind, as well as the body.

Already, the bartender's beady eyes were brimming with panic. A man tied in a chair might think he still had a bargaining chip, something he could use to stay alive. A man on his knees, however, knew his place. This man was feeling all of his possible clever moves melting away.

Asher knew how vital it was for someone to feel important. People talked about food, water, and shelter being necessary for life, but Asher noticed that people clung to a sense of importance with as much desperation as they clung to their last crust of bread.

Just like the body weakened when food was gone, so did the soul wither when a person no longer felt important.

Asher had now struck this man twice. One swift kick to the chest, and one brutal blow to the psyche. Asher had often used the phrase, "this one doesn't matter" with the same force as a good right cross. It was working now. The man babbled, trying to find his place in the world again.

"I can give you money. I can help you. This inn..."

"Shut up," Asher commanded. He didn't have to yell, not anymore. The man's mouth snapped shut. "How about you spend your breath telling me about the men who come to collect money from you?"

The man's eyes sharpened again. There was a wiliness about this one that Asher respected.

"I know that those who send them are capable of sending much worse. So I'm glad to pay my portion and keep my mouth shut."

Asher smiled. The man thought that this was some kind of test. He thought that they were from the Tribulus. Asher toyed with that thought for a moment. He might be able to use that.

No.

This was too early for games. He wanted this sniveling man to know what true danger looked like.

He walked around behind the man and slipped one of his daggers loose, letting the silence do its work.

He gripped the man's pudgy shoulder with one hand and applied the point of the knife, slowly and deliberately. The man yelped and tried to cringe away, but that only made it worse.

"Listen to me," Asher said quietly, leaning his face down to the man's ear. The man only thrashed more, tears and whimpers streamed from his face. Asher pressed harder and felt the point break through the skin. The bartender gasped and although the color drained from his face, he went quiet.

"That's better. It's a different kind of pain, isn't it? The body has one flavor of pain for when danger is near, like a knife pressing on the skin. Then it has a completely different flavor for when damage is actually done. And there would be an entirely new flavor if I had heated the knife first. Isn't it fascinating?"

The bartender nodded, squeezing his eyes shut against the pain.

"Now, let me explain something very clearly. Am I going slowly enough? Can you hear me all right?"

The man whimpered and nodded again.

"Good, good. Sometimes I end up rushing these things, you know. But that won't do when two people need to have an important conversation. Wouldn't you agree?"

More nodding. Asher grunted his approval.

"You seem to think that these men from the Tribulus are dangerous, and I expect that they are. However, we are even more dangerous, aren't we, men?"

Smiles from his crew.

"And we dangerous men have it in mind to get rid of these mongrels from the Tribulus. The good news is that you get to help us. Isn't that exciting?"

Only a whimper now, no nod.

"Yes, very exciting, I know. I was so pleased to

hear how happy you were to pay up and shut up for the Tribulus. Imagine your happiness at fulfilling our requests and perfecting the silence you've only practiced with them. Do we understand each other?"

A vigorous nod.

"I thought so. Sadly, your inn is going to be closed for a while. Repairs and all that. Your kitchen will remain open, however, as we do tend to enjoy a hot meal. It's the little luxuries you miss when you're at war. So we'll be your only guests for the time being, and you will feed us well. Is that all sounding good so far?"

"Yes," the man gasped. Asher approved of the effort. The man was a quick study, learning to breathe through the pain. Breathing was always a key part of pain endurance.

"We'll also need to know everything you know about the Tribulus, including anyone else who might know anything. We'll likely even use you as bait to draw them to us. Any objections to that?"

"None." The man's voice was getting more stable. Asher gave another little dig with the point of his dagger. The man winced, but didn't cringe away like before. There was more iron in this one than his rounded exterior would suggest.

"That's a good answer. We're all in this together, after all. And when this is done, there won't be anything of the Tribulus left. I intend to draw it out, all the way down to the root. Then you won't be troubled any more by these little thugs."

Asher released the man, pulling the knife free. To his credit, the bartender struggled to his feet to look his captors in the eye. Asher smiled. He had recruited his team. They now had a base of operations not connected to any of them, a schedule of hot meals and warm beds, and a reliable source of ongoing information.

It wasn't bad for a day's work.

Chapter 8

It didn't take long to set up shop in the inn. To begin with, there wasn't much inn. Most of the building was one large common room. Along the outer wall, there were a few bedrooms, but they were scarcely more than closets. Asher deduced that most men who entered these rooms did so only after they were drunk and unconscious, and left without whatever coin they had on them for the privilege.

They divided up the rooms. Asher found Vander's bed to be rather luxurious. The man had at least spent some coin on a good mattress and a heavy quilt.

Before turning in, Asher took them all through the plan. Vander's eyes widened at times, but the other two looked almost bored. These were old tricks for the guerrilla fighters. The preparations took only minutes and they were ready.

Old habits came back easily and the men made a schedule for who would be on watch, then each found either their post or a bed. Sleep came quickly for Asher.

A knock so light it could scarcely be heard roused

Asher from his slumber. He rolled out of bed and onto the floor.

Already?

Asher had suspected that closing the inn would draw the attention of the Tribulus, like a farmer seeing one of his plants start to wither. But it had only been a single night. Might one of the customers have reported the odd behavior back to the gang? It seemed unlikely.

More likely, Asher realized, was that Baba had known that this inn was due for collection.

He shook his head. How much more did she know?

He pulled on his shirt and pants and started on the job of lacing up his boots. There was no real need to hurry. Anyone who waited for the enemy to attack was already two steps behind. There was already a plan and two backup plans in place. None of them required Asher to leap about in a panic.

He put his ear to the door, just in case somebody said anything interesting. In this, Asher was disappointed. The two men who came in spoke in crude analogies and threatened the innkeeper, who did a marvelous job simpering and explaining that he would not fall behind in his payments. He only needed a little time. Blah, blah, blah. Asher was impressed by the man's acting. He had potential.

There was a rattle of glass and some laughter. Then the outer door opened and closed. Asher peeked his head out. The innkeeper was still extracting himself from the shelf of glasses they had pushed him into. Luckily, none of the glasses had fallen.

Asher had left nothing to the innkeeper. Instead, he looked to Mendar, who crouched by the edge of the bar. He was visible from Asher's vantage point, but would have been invisible to the other men.

He held up two fingers, then one with a slight hook to it. Asher smiled. There was something glorious about a plan unfolding.

They let the two men get a ways down the street before Mendar and Asher followed. Tormand was left behind to keep an eye on Vander, as well as prepare for the next part of the operation.

Asher and Mendar followed the men from a fair distance, barely keeping them in sight. People tended to travel in straight lines. Once you knew what direction someone was heading, you didn't need to have eyes on them every step of the way. That was, of course, as long as they didn't suspect they were being followed.

No, all they had to do was wait until the men made their next stop, which would be soon. Asher had seen to that.

During the war with the Marauders, Asher had developed a fascination with poisons. One man with a pouch of white powder could massacre an entire company of hardened warriors, as long as he knew where they got their water. Granted, once that was unleashed, it was impossible to pull it back. That village by the river really had been rough.

Asher soon discovered that a more targeted means of poisoning was a simple, concentrated laxative.

There were abundant plants and chemicals that would do the job incredibly well. Even a bit of the soap his wife used for dishes would do the trick. There was nothing better to separate someone from their group.

The intended target would, of their own volition, go off by themselves, and hold in one position for a long time, hours even, until Asher was ready to see to them. Here in town, you even got the added perk that they would lock themselves into a small room, like a package waiting for pickup.

In this case, once the two were separated and distracted, they should be able to quietly collect both men and bring them back to the inn for questioning.

Asher smiled as the taller of the two men began to hold his stomach and walk with a little extra stiffness. The laxative was taking hold even faster than he had anticipated.

Sure enough, the man stopped at the first tavern they came to and ducked inside. His companion waited outside, leaning against a post, his back to them.

Even as he smiled, Asher felt a small twinge of

disappointment. This was going far too quickly. Stephan's guards must be soft. The Tribulus should have been cleaned up long ago.

With a wave, Asher sent Mendar around the building and slowed his own pace. They would converge on the lounging brigand at the same time. Mendar would pop out in front, startling the man and drawing his attention. Asher would move in from behind and they'd have their first Tribulus captive.

Asher pulled his dagger in his left hand, but kept his right hand free. Their primary purpose at this stage was to gather information. If you started swinging blades around, people died, even if by accident.

"Hey!" Mendar popped around the side of the building and shouted. Asher took three quick steps.

And so did the Tribulus thug.

Rather than freezing when Mendar jumped out, the man moved as if he'd been waiting for them, moving quickly out into the street and twisting to get both of them in his sight.

The man smiled when he saw them and settled into a balanced stance, resting on the balls of his feet, ready to jump forward, back, or sideways. He raised a dagger that he had apparently already been holding out of sight.

Asher exchanged glances with Mendar. Did this criminal just smile at them?

Something familiar flared within Asher. This young

pup dared to smirk at him. Asher snarled as the feeling crept up to his teeth. His hands quivered with anticipation. He would see this man broken as he faced a true killer of men. He would hear him whimper to Asher with more ardor than any priest showed his god.

He settled into his stance and saw Mendar do the same out of the corner of his eye. They approached together. Street brawlers would have fanned out to come at the man from two sides. Asher and Mendar had been soldiers together. They moved in formation, close enough to defend and complement each other's efforts. Any skills or training the man had wouldn't matter. Asher and Mendar together could take down any single fighter, regardless of size, strength, or training.

Still, the thug waited for them and grinned wider. That vile smirk made Asher want to break formation, leap forward, and slash a dagger across that face. But discipline prevailed and they advanced as one.

They had about one second's warning before they were attacked, heavy footsteps moving fast behind them.

Asher and Mendar spun as one to see three new men barreling out of the tavern towards them. These three didn't have the polished look of the Tribulus. More likely, they had been hired or pressed into service by the man who had gone in first.

Somehow, the man had realized what was

happening and had turned the ambush back on them.

They split and backpedaled, putting distance between them as the three ruffians rushed to attack. One had been moving in a headlong rush, attempting to tackle Mendar to the ground. With a quick twist, Mendar spun out of the way, ducking under the arm, and punching hard just below the man's ribs on his right side as he passed by. The big man flopped forward like he'd been tripped, and hit the ground without trying to slow his fall.

Even as he dodged his own attacker, Asher felt a teacher's pride as he noted Mendar's flawless precision. There was a point on the right side where a man's liver poked out from beneath the protective rib cage. It was a small target, but if you could hit it with force, it caused excruciating pain. Hit it hard enough, and your opponent's body could shut down like a snuffed candle.

Then Asher had problems of his own as another attacker from the bar closed on him. At the same time, the Tribulus thug attacked Asher from the other side.

Asher moved back quickly, surveying his two opponents. They were nearly opposites. The man from the tavern was older, very large, and was charging forward with a chair leg raised over his head like a club.

The Tribulus man was smaller and held his dagger

low. He was more concerning to Asher than the larger man, however. Rather than charging, he was advancing while in his stance, never a moment off-balance or out of control.

Between the older man's size and the younger one's obvious training, the two of them could give Asher a fair fight.

There was nothing Asher hated more than a fair fight.

He fought to win and he fought to see men break against him, and people didn't break if they thought the fight might turn their way.

Two quick steps moved him straight into the larger man's charge. The brute tried to bring his club down, but Asher was already inside the swing. He wrapped his arms around the man as if to try and lift him off the ground, but continued moving around him like a child swinging around a tree. But Asher's left hand held his dagger, and the swing around the man sliced the blade across his midsection.

The man had only a moment to scream in pain before Asher finished him, plunging his dagger up from behind into the man's back.

Asher's irritation deepened as the Tribulus man continued to advance slowly, unfazed by the display. Asher had won a great many battles against stacked odds by killing one of the attacking group with skill and brutality. It consistently put the rest of the group on their heels, making them too careful. That is, if they didn't break and run then and there.

Asher moved to meet the man, shifting his dagger to his left hand and drawing his sword with his right. The man before him did the same. Asher gripped his dagger firmly. There would be no tricks or thrown daggers this time. Asher had made a mistake, underestimating his opponent the first time around.

Their quiet capture had been ruined. There was no way to undo the attention they'd called to themselves, but they could still come out of this with something to show for it.

It was time to get down to business.

Swords met swords as daggers tried to sneak in, cutting at arms and hands that got too close. New fighters would try for big swings, meant to take off heads and limbs. Or they would try to stab through the body. Those moves had their place, of course, but you weren't likely to get those with an experienced fighter. However, a deep cut on the wrist, a slice of a thumb, or even a solid nick around the knee could quickly drain an opponent of strength. They might fight bravely, but courage is a poor substitute for blood in the veins.

Asher circled until he could see Mendar. He had finished off his second attacker and was now squaring off against the other Tribulus man, who looked uncomfortable, but not as incapacitated by the laxative as he had been acting.

At the moment, Mendar's back was to Asher.

It was a clear signal.

Asher pressed the attack. His opponent was clearly trained, maintaining his balance and keeping his defense tight, but Asher was quicker and more experienced. In the beginning, the man was looking for an opening, a place to attack, but after a few seconds, the man's eyes could see nothing but Asher's flicking sword. His stance weakened as he kept having to move back to avoid Asher's blade. He hissed as Asher's dagger scored a thin line across the back of his knuckles.

Then true fear showed on the man's face as he realized he wasn't going to win this one. He had been cocky going into the fight, and that confidence had carried him through a great start, but now the truth was clear. Asher was the better fighter. If nothing changed, the man would die within a few minutes.

Asher, for his part, had no intention of letting things go even that far.

"Now," he said, then threw back his head and laughed. The man looked confused, though that wouldn't last long.

Mendar took two quick steps back, creating a moment's distance between him and his opponent. He didn't even need to turn to know that Asher had positioned his man just that far behind him.

The turn and the dagger strike were almost casual, like someone turning to put their drink down on a bar. Asher's opponent gasped and his eyes bulged as he felt Mendar's blade slide through his ribs and into his heart. Then those eyes went glassy, the understanding behind them fading.

Asher loved that part.

The remaining Tribulus man had leapt forward once he saw what was happening, but it was far too late. His friend was already on his knees before his blade crossed again with Mendar's. The man's eyes darted side-to-side, looking for some kind of help, or route to escape, but Mendar was pressing his attack hard. If the man turned to run, he'd die.

Still, he looked panicked enough to try it. Asher leaned down to check the man in the dirt. He'd fallen forward on his face, quite dead.

He stood up and walked toward the fight between Mendar and the Tribulus man.

"Enough," Asher said. The man's eyes flicked his way as Asher swung his sword in a back-handed swing. The man narrowly evaded the sword, tripping backwards. It was at that moment that Asher brought his other hand whipping forward, throwing sand that he had scooped up while checking on the dead man.

The sand caught the remaining man full in the face, blinding him. He roared and swung his sword wildly, trying to gain himself a few seconds to clear his eyes.

It wasn't enough, obviously. Asher stepped forward to block one of his wild strikes. At the same time, Mendar swung his sword to where the man's hand would be. The two attacks blended seamlessly and the man's sword fell from his damaged hand.

His will to fight fell with that sword and he slumped to the ground, holding his injured hand and shaking his head side-to-side, as if he could shake the sand clear of his eyes.

Asher gripped his arm and pulled him to his feet. Mendar took the other side, doing a quick check for any more daggers.

Stunned looks followed them from the tavern as they escorted their new prisoner away. Normally, Asher would have enjoyed an audience, but that day, he muttered curses.

So much for stealth.

Chapter 9

Back at their inn, things were already prepared. One of the small rooms had been cleared out and Tormand waited with a chair and ropes.

Mendar grimaced.

"Do we really need to do this?" he asked Asher, low, so only he could hear. "He's not even that good. Half his prisoners die before we learn anything useful. Or they start blabbering anything they think he wants to hear. It's hardly reliable information."

"He is fast," Asher countered.

"We aren't in that big of a hurry," Mendar shot back.

"And he loves his work." Asher smiled. It was true. Moments like this were most of the reason why Tormand worked with Asher. Mendar grimaced.

"You realize that makes it worse, right? Please tell me you realize that, Asher."

"Nonsense." Asher dismissed Mendar's concerns. "A man who enjoys his work will always be the best man for the job. It's not like you're anxious to take his place. I swear, as soon as a man's sword is out of his hands, you lose all of your killer instinct. Why is that?"

Mendar had an answer, but not one he'd like to say to Asher's face, so he stayed quiet instead.

Really, the whole conversation could have been skipped, Mendar had never expected Asher to bend on the issue. But the routine had a notable effect on their prisoner, who had, of course, heard the entire conversation.

He struggled against their hold, but a small dig with the point of a dagger put a quick stop to any escape efforts. Still, the man tried to slow their advance as they dragged him towards a grinning Tormand.

"Be careful," Asher warned. "This is the one who took the laxative."

They wrestled him into a chair and Tormand tied the man, quickly and efficiently. There was no gag. Tormand disapproved of them entirely.

Asher and Mendar left the room, closing the door firmly behind them.

Mendar hoped the man would break quickly. He had done what he could to nudge him along his way. It would go much better for him long-term if he didn't fight the process. Mendar had seen many of Tormand's subjects after he was done. The lucky ones were dead.

Mendar turned to the door. He didn't want to be around once the screaming started.

"Asher?" Tormand called from the small room.

Mendar turned back, curious. "You're going to want to see this!"

Mendar hurried back as Asher pushed into the cramped room. Tormand had lashed the man's head to his knees with thin cords digging into the man's neck. His shirt had been stripped away.

It didn't take a second look to see what had captured Tormand's attention. A puffy, pink scar ran along the man's shoulder, just below the bone ridge. It was about a hand's breadth wide and perfectly matched the one on Mendar's shoulder, on Tormand's shoulder, and every other member of Asher's elite squad.

"Show me his face," Asher commanded. Tormand was already shaking his head.

"He's not one of us. Do you really think all three of us would have missed such a thing?"

"Could it be an accident?" Mendar asked. "Scars aren't that hard to come by, especially for someone in his business."

"A scar that size, perfectly straight, and in that location? What could have caused that? Any chance blow would have been jagged, or at more of an angle," Tormand responded.

Asher's face hardened.

"Find out everything he knows. I'm going to talk to Baba."

"Again with the Trash Lady?" Tormand sneered in disgust. "Bring cloth plugs for your nose."

Asher ignored the barb. Oddly enough, he knew that Baba wouldn't appreciate him defending her. He knew better than anyone how carefully Baba crafted her image. She would have smiled at Tormand's insult. One more dupe who couldn't see past a thin layer of grime.

"I'm coming along," Mendar said. Asher raised an eyebrow, but didn't object. In a way, it was Mendar's right to be at Asher's side. He had certainly saved his life often enough. He also carried more of Asher's secrets than anyone else in the world.

Asher set a quick pace as they set off. Somewhere behind them, a man started screaming. Tormand would have a very thorough report for them when they got back.

"We know it's not one of our men," Mendar started out.

"We know no such thing!" Asher snapped, his frustration erupting from his outwardly quiet demeanor. "You watched them fight, saw the training. We should have suspected one of us even before we saw the scar."

"None of your squad would betray you!" Mendar insisted.

"Why not?" Asher countered. "I taught all of you to survive, to win at all costs. That fits everything we've heard about the Tribulus. Besides, would they even see it as betraying me? They don't know I'm after them. Not yet, at least, though I suspect there will be rumors after our little display by the tavern."

"I still don't believe it," Mendar responded stubbornly. "We fought warriors! We didn't bully fat merchants."

Mendar paused as he considered their actions of the previous day.

"Ok, so we bullied one fat merchant on this job, but that's certainly not who we are!"

"People change," Asher muttered. Mendar shook his head all the more.

"Not this much. I couldn't imagine using your teachings, your fighting style, to create something so..."

"...effective?" Asher finished for him. "I know how you want to see the world, Mendar. You want your friends to be good and your enemies to be evil, but life isn't that simple. How long has it been since you've seen the members of the old squad? I haven't seen most of them in nearly three years."

"Three years?" Mendar was aghast. "You haven't kept in touch with them? I've tried to see each of them every couple months or so."

"Why?"

"Why? Asher, I mean no disrespect, but what is wrong with you? These men were your friends! We bled together!"

"And the Marauders bled right along with us. Should I feel some special bond with them? What if I did go visit with the old squad? Would we tell stories of old times? I want those stories forgotten. Or perhaps we'd discuss farming. If there's anything I hate more than farming, it's talking about farming."

They walked in silence for a while after that. Mendar was having to rethink some of his most fundamental views. For him, Asher's squad had been closer to him than his own brothers. Could Asher really feel nothing for them? No. Mendar refused to believe it. Therefore, it must be as Asher said. He avoided them to keep the stories from spreading. Or, he kept away to separate them from Eliana.

It was one of the great truths of the squad: Eliana was to know nothing about what Asher did. Only Mendar had even met her, and that had been a chance meeting. Even after what he said, Mendar still believed, absolutely, that Asher was loyal to his men, that he would do anything for them. However, he knew that any loyalty Asher felt for his men was a mere candle next to the blazing sun that was his loyalty to Eliana. Once, one of the men had joked that Asher would kill all of them before letting Eliana stub her toe.

No one had laughed.

That made sense to Mendar and the world spun on in the right direction again. Yes, Asher loved his men, but he would keep away from them to protect Eliana. That made sense.

Asher's mind, it seemed, had been on other thoughts.

"Who lives closest to here?"

"What?"

"You said you kept in touch with the men. Who lives closest to here? Maybe we don't need Baba to start getting some information."

"You want to question the men?" Mendar asked, incredulous.

"Listen, there's a connection here. Fine, maybe none of our old squad is involved, but there's still a connection. The sooner we get to the bottom of this, the sooner you can prove it was all perfectly innocent."

Mendar sighed, unable to argue the facts.

"Who is closest?" Asher pressed. There was a plan now, and this personal connection had only sharpened his focus. If it was one of his men, that meant they were up against a truly dangerous adversary, not just some boss thug.

"Largan," Mendar said miserably. It felt like a small betrayal. "He ran into some bad luck after separating from his wife. He lives in a shanty in this area."

He guided Asher down to a sprawl of shacks, right by the river. This part of town was where things got really desperate. Here, there were no inns or taverns, seedy or otherwise. There had to be at least a little money to attract a business. Here, there were only the lost and broken. Asher frowned. Was Largan really living here?

Asher truly hadn't kept in touch with most of his squad when he went off to fight his private war against the Marauders. There were a few, like Mendar, who had helped out here and there, but most of them had folded back into the regular army.

When Asher had returned home, he had checked in on some of them, but only once. At that time, Largan had seemed the happiest among them, smiling at his wife as she smiled back.

Chapter 10

"What happened here?" Asher asked, looking at the slumping lean-to they were about to enter. Mendar didn't need any clarification on the question.

"The nightmares never stopped for Largan. He held on for as long as he could, pretending, but he started sleeping less and less. Before the first year passed, he wasn't himself any more. He started drinking, but that made it worse. Then, one day, he hit Leah during an argument. After that, he moved out and hasn't been back since. I think he's afraid."

Asher had heard of soldiers like that, but he could never quite understand, himself. He had never had nightmares. Oh, he had dreams where there were enemies, even monsters, but in those dreams, he fought and won. Sometimes, he would wake up panting, exhilarated.

As far as hitting his wife, what sort of man would do that? Were there no other enemies for him to attack? Asher remembered Largan's wife. She was a strong woman, but she was no Marauder. Where was the victory in striking one's own?

Asher wrinkled his nose and ducked into the lean-to. A large lump lay motionless on a mat in the back corner, likely the only corner that didn't get wet when it rained.

Asher sneered in disgust, walked over, and kicked at the prone figure.

Instantly, he knew he had made a mistake. There was no grunt, no resistance from a body in the blankets. There were only blankets.

He threw himself to the side, but it was too late. Largan dropped on him from above. Coming into the dark space from the bright sunshine had made him blind to Largan tucked up on a small ledge, ready to pounce on intruders.

Largan hit into him like a pouncing cat, gripping and clawing, bearing Asher to the ground.

Asher twisted and tried to get a hold of a wrist, an ankle, anything he could use to leverage his way out. Nothing worked. Largan was like a wild thing, moving in an aggressive scramble. He didn't even plant his feet in the ground to get leverage, his feet wrapped around Asher as he kicked savagely backwards with his heels over and over again. Each strike did little damage, but neither could Asher see his way out.

Then teeth clamped down on his arm.

He roared and kicked hard against the lean-to wall, hoping to use the momentum to roll both of them, hopefully with Largan ending up on bottom. That was Asher's second mistake in under five seconds. The wall he kicked was not the wall of the building, but the structure of the lean-to.

It groaned hideously as Asher's kick knocked one of the primary support beams clear of the ground. Large boards which suddenly didn't fit snugly against the roof started falling down around them. One hit Asher's leg and he roared in pain. Another hit Largan in the ribs and he rolled free of Asher, dodging away from this new attack.

Then strong hands took hold of Asher, dragging him clear of the rickety structure, which seemed to be falling apart, one piece at a time.

Largan made it out before they did, hitting and rolling clear of the wreckage in a surprisingly smooth maneuver.

He tried to rub dirt away from his bloodshot eyes, but that only made it worse. He still came out in a perfect stance, Asher noted. While the man looked, and smelled, like a swamp animal, there were clearly some lessons he hadn't forgotten.

"Largan, stop!" Asher barked. Perhaps his stance wasn't the only thing Largan remembered from his soldier days.

Sure enough, Largan stopped abruptly.

"Asher?" he asked in a voice barely above a whisper. His shoulders slumped. "Have you come to kill me?"

"Do you need killing?" Asher responded with a question of his own.

Largan's ready stance sagged, as if weight were

suddenly piling on his shoulders. His hands dropped.

"I don't know," Largan shrugged. "Maybe. I don't see a way out. Every night I tell myself that I want to die. But also every night, I set traps, fake trails, and do everything I can to stay safe. Would I really go through all that trouble if I wanted to die?"

It wasn't a real question. Largan ran through the words like he had rehearsed them over and over in his mind. There was a calmness to the words that didn't match his haggard appearance or the tortured look behind his wild eyes.

"You." The piercing eyes focused on Asher, really seeing him this time. "You always showed up when we needed you. You were always there to kill the ones we couldn't take care of ourselves. Are you here now to finish what I've started? I'll fight you. I don't think I can just sit here. You wouldn't want that anyway. You'll win, of course. You always win, don't you? Then I'll be dead and I won't have to do this any more."

Largan's voice had become more frantic the further he worked his way through his mad plea. Asher found himself considering it. How else would this end? One cold night, Largan would drink too much, pass out, and freeze to death by morning. Maybe it would be a mercy to let him die as a soldier. Asher's fingers idly played over the handle of his sword. Largan would be expecting the thrown dagger, but maybe there was another trick he could

70

use.

Largan fixed his stance, his hands raising.

Mendar sprang forward.

"Largan! Asher has a job. We're taking care of something for King Stephan. Why don't you get cleaned up and join us?"

Asher grunted. He didn't really need or want more men on this job. Even if he did, he wouldn't have chosen Largan, and certainly not in his present state. Still, what would he say to Mendar? That he'd rather just kill the poor wretch and be done with it? Besides, now that Mendar had blurted out they were working for the king, Asher would have to keep an eye on him.

No, there was nothing for it. Asher nodded and waved Largan forward. The man obeyed. Mere seconds ago, he had been ready to jump into a fight he was sure would end in his death. Now, Mendar had tossed him the smallest table scrap of hope and now he followed meekly, like a whimpering dog.

"Take him back to the inn," Asher ordered Mendar. "Get him cleaned up."

Asher was happy to see them go. He didn't want to look at Largan anymore. In fact, he didn't want to see Mendar, either. Asher might have imagined it, but he could swear he saw accusation in Mendar's gray eyes.

Chapter 11

"For the last time, I'm fine," Eliana insisted to Rachel, Ander's wife. "Walking relaxes me. I'll stay within sight of the house."

"If you'll wait long enough for me to get this bread in the oven, I'll go with you. I could use the exercise. Or take one of the boys."

Eliana searched for some reason why she couldn't wait, or some excuse not to take one of the boys. Rachel was one of those women who managed to be everywhere at once.

Eliana couldn't figure out how she did it. How could she care for her two boys, run the household, and even manage her large garden, but still somehow be right at Eliana's side every minute of every day?

She didn't even feel much like a walk, she was more and more tired these days, but if she didn't get a moment to herself, she thought she might scream.

The first couple days here had been so pleasant. Asher didn't like company, so most days at their farm were oppressively quiet. So being here in this warm and lively home had been like the sunshine of summer. However, Eliana soon realized that a summer's heat could be stifling.

Ander was always asking how she felt, multiple times every hour. Rachel didn't even ask, she jumped in and did things to make Eliana more comfortable, whether she had asked for it or not. Then there were the two boys. Simeon, the oldest, was mostly quiet, but when he did speak, it was always to ask questions that Eliana struggled to answer.

Eliana's mother had died while she was very young, and her father hadn't thought it important that his daughter get much in the way of education. She had always felt a little self-conscious about not knowing much about the world and how it worked. Simeon, unfortunately, had decided that since she came from somewhere else, she must know things he didn't.

"Why do sparks from the fire float upwards, when everything else falls down?"

"If trees grow from the soil, why aren't there empty spots in the soil around them?"

"How will the baby get out of your belly?"

Eliana hadn't been able or, in some cases, willing to answer his questions. He remained undeterred, however, whenever she told him she didn't know, or when his mother shooed him away. He would always circle back with some new line of questioning, trying to figure out what expertise Eliana was hiding from him.

The only one in the house who didn't pester her was little Joseph, but that was because he didn't show any interest in her at all. He only followed Simeon around, inserting himself into whatever his older brother was doing. It was a singular focus, and Eliana suspected he didn't see much of what else happened around him.

"You know, I noticed that the clothes on the line are dry," Eliana pointed out, a brilliant idea occurring to her. "Maybe I should bring those in and fold them while you get the bread in the oven."

Rachel looked horrified at the thought of her pregnant house-guest doing manual labor.

"Don't you dare!" she exclaimed. "You go ahead on your walk, I'll send one of the boys along when they come in."

"Are you sure?" Eliana asked, fighting her smile down. "It's really no trouble."

"Go!" Rachel insisted, going so far as to walk towards her, waving her away with her flour-covered hands.

Eliana walked out into the fresh air and made for the treeline. The boys were behind the house, so as long as she kept the house between her and them, they wouldn't see her and think to follow.

She sighed with her whole body as the trees closed in behind her, cutting her off from the house and its overly friendly occupants. She slowed her walk, more careful now of her bulging belly and her questionable balance.

She angled off to her right, planning on making a large loop around the house. She caught glimpses of fur as little animals scurried away. She stopped in a small clearing to lean against a tree and rest. She didn't quite dare sit down. Standing back up was quite the chore, and lately it caused a sharp pain down by her waist whenever she bent over. The old mothers had all assured her that random aches and pains were a normal part of pregnancy, so she didn't worry too much about it.

"Hello."

She jumped as a man stepped out on the other side of the clearing. He immediately raised a hand and apologized. "Sorry to scare you. I'll stay over here. I'm actually a friend of your husband's."

Eliana's gaze narrowed, though the man kept his word and stayed on the far side of the clearing. The man's clothes were fine cotton. His boots came up to his knees, the black leather shone from endless polishing. He wore his hair slicked back, the ends hanging down to his shoulders. In many ways, he reminded her of Asher, though he lacked her husband's bearing.

"My husband doesn't have friends," she stated simply.

It came out sounding harsher than she intended, but it was true. The closest thing Asher had to a friend was Mendar, but she had seen them together and "friendship" was the wrong word for their relationship. Mendar obeyed Asher. Eliana didn't maintain many friendships, herself, but she was pretty sure friendship wasn't about obedience.

The man across the clearing laughed as if she had made some great joke.

"I suppose you're right. Asher doesn't really do friends, does he?"

"No. So who are you?" Eliana pressed. Even lounging twenty paces away, the man managed to look like he was looming over her.

"But he does do enemies, doesn't he?" The man continued as if he hadn't heard her question.

"My husband doesn't have enemies," Eliana replied.

"Oh?" the man responded, showing genuine surprise. "And what if I said I was one such enemy?"

"Then I shouldn't be talking to you."

"Too scary?" The man smirked and leaned forward.

"No." In truth, Eliana's knees felt weak and she felt like screaming, but she'd lived on a farm her whole life, long enough to know you didn't turn your back on a growling dog. "Like I said, my husband doesn't have enemies, only dead men. If you're his enemy, then you should know better than to bother the living."

The man's grin froze for a moment and he blinked a couple times before regaining his composure.

"You think your husband is that dangerous, do you? What have you heard?"

"During the war, I volunteered in some of the recovery tents. Nothing serious, just cleaning. But I did talk to some of the wounded men. Once, a group of them started talking about who was the deadliest fighter in the army."

"Oh, and they said it was Asher?" the man asked, a sneer in his voice. "What would common soldiers know of such things?"

"No. They said it was Mendar."

The man's smile cracked, his jaw tightening.

"Then, after the war, I met Mendar. And the man jumps when my husband barks. So, either my husband commands dangerous men, or he is more dangerous than them all. In either case, all I have to do is mention that you were here. How many men would kill you just to win my husband's goodwill?"

The smiling taunt was gone now. The man took two steps forward, snarling.

"Don't do that." A small voice spoke from the other side of the tree Eliana had been leaning on. The man drew up, a smile once again on his face.

"Aww! Look at that! You have yourself a little defender. And what's your name, boy?"

Eliana clenched her fists to keep them from trembling, but it didn't work. She had already been certain the man was going to harm her when he had started walking forward. Now, Ander's son was in danger, as well.

"I am Simeon, son of Ander. You are not allowed on our land."

"Is that so, son of Ander? And who is Ander? Some farmer? One more man with his nostrils full of dirt? What is that to me, child?"

"My father is a good man." Against all reason, Simeon's calm, logical tone was soothing Eliana's nerves. How on earth could the young boy be so serene at a time like this? The man across the clearing looked around quickly, also a little unnerved by the young man's stoic features.

"So? Good men die as fast as bad men, often faster."

"That is true." Simeon nodded as if they were discussing the weather, and not the death of his father. He continued calmly.

"The difference is that when a good man dies, there are people who miss him. You see, a good man wins the respect and the help of friends, colleagues," the boy mused, pausing meaningfully, "even neighbors."

"Neighbors?" The man looked around again, taking a step back towards the trees. "What are you babbling about, boy?"

Simeon took a step forward, as if trying to corner the much larger man.

"What could I be talking about?" he challenged. "A neighbor who might stop by to check in? A farmer who knows his own land well enough to be suspicious about a strange footprint? Maybe men smart enough to send a distraction long enough for them to close off routes of escape? A boy, perhaps?"

Simeon's eyes flicked to the man's left.

"Wait!" he yelped, throwing out his hand. "Not yet!"

A branch cracked in the forest. The man didn't even pause to look toward the sound. With a soldier's reflexes in an ambush, he bolted, running away from the sound and out of the clearing.

"We should go." Simeon grabbed Eliana's hand and pulled her back towards the house.

"If it's all the same to you, I'll wait for your father, I think I need some help getting back."

"My father isn't here, he's still out in the field. I don't think we should wait around, though. That man might soon figure out that no one is following him."

"No one?" Eliana looked toward where the branch had snapped. She could now see little Joseph, waving a large stick as best he could, smacking another tree with it. "Oh, no!"

Sickening comprehension settled into Eliana's stomach. The thought of the man coming back gave strength to her legs. She could imagine how furious the man would be if he discovered he'd been fooled by two little boys and a branch.

She stared unbelievingly at Simeon. She hadn't known many children, but there was definitely something wrong with this one.

By the time they made it back to the house, Eliana was leaning heavily on Simeon, who struggled, but never complained. Joseph trailed behind, still whacking things with his stick, largely oblivious to Eliana's struggle.

She settled down in a chair and wished her husband were there with her.

That night, contractions started and a fever struck.

Chapter 12

The walk to Baba's cleared Asher's head. His mind was always busy, his eyes flickering to every rooftop and dark alley. It was somehow calming, a way of taking control of his world. Here he stalked. Here he was feared. No one would dare...

"So?" a voice said by his elbow.

Asher jumped. He spun on Baba.

"What are you doing, you filthy rag of a woman!" How did she do that? Asher's heart was pounding. He felt angry at himself. He'd been so focused on checking for every danger that he hadn't been considering the most obvious. Naturally, he took his anger out on Baba.

"One of these days, you're going to get stabbed, you wretch! And it's going to be me that does it. I know you do it on purpose. It's some sick power play. Well, congratulations, you got me. Does it make you happy?"

"A little." Baba smiled under the force of his tirade, undisturbed by his anger and threats. "Most people aren't worth the effort."

"I'm glad you consider me worthy," Asher

snapped, but his anger was already dying away. There was no point in being mad at Baba. She found most anger amusing, proof that she was controlling the direction of the conversation.

"How is your investigation going?" Baba returned the topic to what she wanted to discuss. "Have you rooted out the Tribulus yet?"

"We have a prisoner,"Asher reported, continuing to stroll along the street as Baba shuffled along beside him. "Tormand is with him now."

"Poor sod," Baba muttered. "That man enjoys his work far too much."

"He'll find out everything soon enough, but there's already a deeper mystery."

"Oh?" Baba prompted when Asher fell silent. Asher did this entirely to get back at her for besting him. She might be above nearly all regular human impulses, but her desire to know secrets was a driving, primal force.

"A scar, the same as my men carry."

"Right shoulder, below the ridge?" she asked. Asher nodded, not surprised that she already knew what he was talking about.

Asher had never recruited her, at least not in the classic sense. He and his squad had been wrapped in secrets, both during and after the war. So, she had sought him out, had studied him from afar until she couldn't learn any more without talking with him herself.

He was a wealth of secrets and he drew her like a moth to a flame.

"Mendar insists it couldn't be any of my squad, but the connection is undeniable. Even the lowly thugs sent to intimidate my pet innkeeper knew how to fight, and well."

"Tell me about the scar." Her eyes glittered with anticipation. This was one of the secrets Asher had made her wait for. Once she knew all his secrets, she would likely disappear, so he made sure to keep back a few choice morsels. This was one such morsel.

"I trained my men to fight, but I also taught them tactics. I taught them how to attack minds, and how to control their own. When their training was completed, I would bring each of them out into the woods, alone.

"Then, I would order them to make no move, and make no sound. I would make them promise to obey."

"And once they promised?" Baba urged. He hadn't even paused in his story, but she was leaning forward, staring into his eyes as if she could draw the very memories from them.

"I would beat them, savagely, until they could no longer stand or kneel. Then, my knee in their back, I would carve a line on their shoulder, moving the knife as slowly as I could."

Baba shivered, giving him an odd grin.

"All of your men have been through this experience?"

"All of them," Asher confirmed. "All of them bear the scar."

"And you really think that someone who obeyed you through such a thing would turn on you now?"

"I've already been over this with Mendar," Asher said. "Maybe they don't see it as turning against me."

"It would still be turning against the kingdom and against Stephan. I know you don't like him, but I happen to know that most of your men joined the army because they believed in him and his cause."

"Men can change, especially when they get desperate," Asher insisted.

"More desperate than being beaten and tortured by their own captain and mentor?"

Asher humphed. He had to admit, it didn't sound very likely, the more he talked about it. Still, there was a connection.

"How many went through this training?"

"Well, there were a total of thirty in the squad."

"That's not what I asked."

Asher paused. He had only been considering those who passed. There had been some who screamed or fought back during the final test. Asher had dismissed them and they had slunk off as cowards and oath-breakers. Asher hadn't given them another thought. He said as much to Baba.

"Nobody looks at trash." She nodded like an old sage. "You assumed that their weakness, as you saw it, would send them down a path of mediocrity and degradation, right?"

"I hadn't thought about it in such big words, but I suppose you're right."

"But the fact is, there are men out there that you trained that were never part of your squad. Why couldn't it be one of them?"

Asher had to admit that he liked that option better than it being one of his own men. If nothing else, he wouldn't have to see Mendar's accusing eyes as they investigated each member of the old squad.

"Any idea where to find them?" Asher asked. Baba considered for a long moment.

"It took me quite a while to gather all the names of the members of your crew. Like you, I hadn't put much thought into those who washed out. Still, if there's one thing the army is good at, it's writing down names. Every man who was excused from regular duty to train for your squad had to be accounted for. There would be records somewhere."

Asher scowled. He didn't like his options. Baba, had, apparently, seen the same ones.

"That shouldn't be a problem, right? You can go and ask your buddy, Stephan. I'm sure he's as anxious as you to have this thing finished."

"I'm not about to go and point the king's attention to my men. Even if it isn't one of them, he's not dumb enough to ignore that each could be a threat. Why, if it was one of the scrubs that built the Tribulus, it would stand to reason that one of the actual elite could do an even better job, create an organization that Stephan wouldn't even know about."

"I'm not sure he'd see it that way." Baba mused.

"I don't care," Asher retorted. "We can't let this become a matter of my men causing trouble. I'd never be rid of him. He'd be checking in every time a hen went missing. No, we need to get the information some other way."

"As you like." Baba spread her hands in acquiescence. Each fingernail was nearly black with grime. Everything you could see on Baba was grimy, though Asher noted that her teeth were always clean. "I will look into where those records are kept, or who else might know something, but you should start by talking with your own men. Surely some of them remember those they trained with. Not everybody discards people once they cease to be useful."

Asher raised an eyebrow, but he could tell Baba meant nothing bad by it. Baba generally didn't judge people, though it wasn't out of the purity of her heart. Rather, she didn't really care what other people did. She studied them like a child studying an ant hill. You didn't judge an ant because it acted differently from the others, you just marked it as a fascinating oddity.

Chapter 13

Back at the inn, Largan had cleaned up, even shaved, and was looking more like the man Asher remembered, though he had the disturbing tendency to stare off into space whenever he thought no one was watching.

Tormand had cleaned up and was sitting back in a chair, looking proud of himself. He sat up as Asher came in the door, ready to report on what he had learned from their prisoner.

Asher raised a hand and stopped him.

"It can wait until morning."

Tormand's face fell, but Asher felt exhausted. He also knew himself well enough to know that if he got new information at this point, he wouldn't be able to sleep for turning it over and over in his mind.

The watch was even easier to schedule with Largan in the mix, though Asher didn't know if the man could be relied upon.

Still, he reflected, the man had been ready for him when Asher had come into his lean-to. He might not have his head in the right place, but his paranoia was stronger than ever.

Asher found his bed and fell asleep. He woke up in the morning, checked his weapons, got dressed, and headed back out to the common area. The rest of his men were already waiting for him, as was a simple breakfast of leftover stew.

"Report," Asher commanded Tormand, once he had shot a glare at Vander and settled down at the table to eat his mushy meal.

"I'll start with what he didn't know. He doesn't know who's in charge of the whole organization, or who set up the training routine. They are given the cut at the end of their training, but there's no beating, and no oath to hold still and stay quiet."

Tormand managed to put a sneer into his voice that communicated exactly what he thought of such milkwater half-measures.

"Each batch of recruits are trained by a few of the older members, each one contributing their own specialty. They recruit almost exclusively orphans and men without families. The Tribulus is supposed to be their family."

"It also removes a lot of distractions and leverage points," Asher noted.

"Indeed," Tormand agreed, then continued. "They've been operating for around four years. Our little pup back there has been with them around two years now. They operate all over the city and even have a couple rackets going on farms in the country."

"Four years?" Largan spoke up for the first time.

"That means they got started before the war was over."

"War is a profitable business," Asher mused. "I guess somebody felt like getting a head start."

"Their organization is divided into regions," Tormand continued his report. "Each region knows very little about the others, and all of them report to a central authority, though the one you brought me wasn't up the ladder enough for direct communication with the high and mighty."

"So, where is..." Asher started, then stopped as there was a loud knock at the front door of the inn.

"We're closed!" Vander called out. Asher turned. He had honestly forgotten the man was there. It was easy to forget an innkeeper.

"I'm looking for Asher!" A reedy voice called out. The group exchanged glances. Asher shot an especially dark look at the innkeeper.

"Who have you told that we're here?"

"No one!" The innkeeper broke out in a sweat immediately. "You can ask your own men! I haven't even left the inn since you came."

Asher waved aside his begging.

"You be Asher." He pointed to Tormand, who was already lounging, facing the front of the building. Mendar and Asher moved to both sides of the door. Largan grabbed a broom and started sweeping dirt back and forth. Asher nodded to the innkeeper, who hustled around the bar to open the door.

"Come in and be quick about it," the innkeeper snapped at the newcomer.

A man walked in, leaning on a cane. He wasn't that old, but there was something unnatural about the way his right leg bent when he walked.

He stepped forward, peering at Tormand.

"You're not Asher," he declared. "I need to talk with Asher."

"Sit down." Asher commanded the man from behind. "And put the cane on the table."

The man jumped a little at Asher's tone, but quickly obeyed. Asher circled the man, looking him over.

"How did you know it wasn't me?"

"I knew you," the man stammered, then quickly corrected himself. "That is to say, I saw you when you were in the army. I was flag bearer for a month or so before a war horse kicked my leg and busted my knee all to pieces. It never did heal back the way it was."

"How did you know I was here?" Asher pressed, trying to move past the man's war stories.

"Oh, I live right across the street there. I've known you were here the whole time, I just couldn't figure why. Then, earlier today, people started talking about somebody taking on the Tribulus. Then it all made sense. You're here to clean them out, aren't you?"

Asher growled. He had hoped to get a little further than a street brawl before tipping their hand.

"Who else knows we're here?" He was standing now, fists on the table. The man leaned back in his chair.

"Nobody! At least, nobody that I know of. I only came because I need your help. And now I know you're helping people, I thought..."

Whatever his thought was, it died on his tongue as Asher stared down at him.

"Here is the help I offer you," Asher growled the words. "In exchange for your silence and a promise not to come back to this place, I will let you leave here alive. How does that sound?"

The man nodded, gulping.

"Tormand, please add your own help to our friend's departure."

Tormand leapt to his feet, grabbing the man's cane off the table. He proceeded to chase the man out of the inn. The man mostly hopped on one leg as Tormand swatted at him with his own cane. Once the man was out of the inn, Tormand threw the cane after him before closing the door and returning to his seat.

Chapter 14

"Something is wrong."

Chapter 15

"You should have let me kill him, or at least question him," Tormand threw out as he settled back into his seat. "He could have been a spy."

"Believe it or not, I remember the man," Asher replied. "I remember wondering if he was brave, stupid, or both. He would charge with the army carrying that stupid flag as if it were both shield and spear. It doesn't surprise me that he was injured, though I would have expected a Marauder's blade before a horse's hoof."

"Fortune always favors the stupid," Tormand mused. "It's little wonder he finds himself in trouble now. Luck always runs out."

"True enough," Mendar muttered, in a rare moment of agreement with Tormand. "I wonder what he wanted. He had to know it was dangerous to come here."

"It doesn't matter," Asher reminded everyone. "We need to stay focused on the job. If the limping flag-bearer recognized us and was able to trace us here, it won't be long before the Tribulus has our location. We need to move fast."

"And where are we moving to?" Mendar asked.

"We follow Tormand's lead. Our original plan hasn't changed. We work our way up the chain until we can draw out whoever is running this operation. Then we bring his head or their heads to Stephan. We retire publicly as heroes."

Uneasy silence greeted him.

"What is it?" he asked.

Tormand cleared his throat.

"Does it really need to be our last job? I've gotta say, I'm not as excited as you might think to go back to killing animals day in and day out."

"I already retired as a hero once." Largan looked at Asher's chest as he spoke, not meeting his eyes. "I messed it all up. I don't see it going any better the second time around."

"I can understand that," Asher mused, then turned to Mendar. "What about you? You enjoy your work. I imagine you're anxious to get back. Why so quiet?"

Mendar shifted in his seat.

"It's like this, Asher. Sometimes, when I notice that a tool hasn't been used for a while, I'll make something that uses that tool, just so it gets some use and I don't lose the knack. Fighting those men today felt like that. We went through so much during the war. We trained so hard, sacrificed so much to become the best. And we were the best!"

Mendar stood, becoming animated in his speech.

"Yes, I love woodworking, and I love coming home to my family every single night. But we were something special, a force in the world. Now we have to sit in the harness as good dogs and forget that we were wolves? Where do we fit now?"

Asher felt hollow hearing the words. They were his own thoughts, spoken out loud. It was particularly jarring hearing them from Mendar. More than anyone, Mendar had seemed to adapt and thrive in his new life. Hearing that even he shared Asher's frustration hinted that there was no good answer.

"I don't know!" Asher snapped, with more bitterness than he intended to show. He moderated his tone and continued. "I have no intention of becoming one of King Stephan's guards. I don't see myself doing any better under his structure than I did in his regular army. Nor do I intend to go the way of the Tribulus. So what is left?"

He looked around, part of him hoping that one of them had an answer he hadn't seen. All were quiet, so he continued.

"Even raiding the Marauders would gain little returns. Their lifestyle doesn't lead to gathering much wealth. Besides, I hear there's a sickness going around there, best to stay clear.

"No, there's nothing left. There is nothing for us but to find our new places in life. I taught each of you to be adaptable. Adapt now. Acquire whatever new skills you need."

"Like you?" Tormand shot back. "You dress awfully fine for a farmer. Would you have us believe that you're happy grubbing in the dirt?"

"I am happy," Asher growled at him, then abruptly realized the mismatch between words and tone. Even Mendar cracked a smile at someone snarling about their happiness.

"Maybe you are happy," Mendar cut in, playing peacemaker once again. "But we all know that any happiness you've got comes from your wife, not your mediocre farm. That thing has more rocks than sprouts. All we're asking is that, when this job is through, you talk to Stephan. Maybe he'd have use for a squad like ours. The Tribulus can't be the only thing adding pressure to his royal head. He might talk all high and mighty, but any ruler needs a reliable way to make problems disappear. Could Stephan really be so different?"

Asher honestly wasn't sure. There was an odd earnestness about the man. He really believed the drivel he spouted about justice and the rule of law. Asher would have called him nearly incorruptible, if he himself weren't, even now, working as an assassin on the king's orders.

"I'll talk to him," Asher agreed. The men all exchanged smiles, especially Largan, who exhaled as if he had been holding his breath.

Inwardly, Asher grimaced. He had no real intention of talking to King Stephan. The man was too clever by half. If Asher and his squad started working for the king, even in a small capacity, it would only be a matter of time before he controlled them, body and soul. Asher wouldn't stand for that.

"Take us to the local center," Asher commanded Tormand. "Largan, you come, too. We shouldn't underestimate these people. From now on, nobody goes off on their own. Preferably, we stick together, when possible."

"What about the innkeeper? Don't we need to leave someone to watch him?"

Four sets of eyes turned on Vander, who shrank under the sudden scrutiny. Asher considered him a moment.

"I believe that his window for betraying us has passed. If they know where we are already, there's no way he'll convince them he wasn't helping willingly. They'll kill him. And if any of us are captured, let's all agree now to beg them for his life and insist he had nothing to do with it."

All of his men grinned at the thought. There were few better ways of convincing someone of something than to vigorously deny that thing. Vander seemed to realize the same thing and went a little paler. He stood to speak, though.

"You're right, Asher. I'm in this now, whether I like it or not. If there's anything else I can do, just let me know. I only win here if you do."

"A fine speech, wasn't it men?" Asher quipped.

Tormand gave a little chuckle. "But I think he's got the idea. Leave him. He'll be here when we get back."

The men were happy to comply. The hope that they might be able to continue working as a team had put a spring in their step and a little extra steel in their eyes. As they moved out onto the street, they fell naturally into formation, as if it had only been days since they had patrolled together, instead of years.

People saw them coming and moved off of the street. Asher couldn't help but smile. People recognized danger on a primal level. Each member of the team brought their own flavor to the mix. Asher's intensity, Mendar's watchfulness, Tormand's dead eyes, and even Largan's instability all added to the sense that this was a group that could start killing people at any moment.

Asher would miss this, he knew.

Chapter 16

The walk to the building was surprisingly short, less than a mile. It was a warehouse, one still in active use, by the looks of things.

"Largan and Tormand, you fan right and cover any other exits. Mendar, you're with me. Don't worry about prisoners until we're down to the last few."

"Understood," Mendar said flatly. He was focused now. When things got really serious, there was a part of Mendar that shut down and he went cold inside.

Largan and Tormand disappeared around the side of the building. That was enough of a head start.

Asher drew sword and dagger, quickening his step. He was nearly running when he hit the door with a powerful forward kick. The wood split and burst inward. The recoil from the door halted Asher's momentum, but not Mendar's. He shot through the door before the splinters were done falling.

Asher hurried through the door, just in time to see Mendar pulling his dagger out of a guard who had been sitting by the door. The man had only made it half-way to standing before Mendar ended him.

Then Asher was moving into the room, moving

nearly at a run. Chairs clattered as men scrambled to their feet. Asher made it to them first, killing two as they tried to pull their swords. The third actually got his sword free of leather before Asher swatted it aside with his own sword, following his momentum into the man, stabbing upward with his dagger as he bowled the man over, running him into the man behind him.

Less than five seconds had passed, and four men were dead. Mendar continued around the border of the room, where other guards were leaving their posts by the door to move to the table, where Asher was shredding through the chaos of men.

As their focus was on Asher, they didn't see Mendar running up behind them, getting to them before they could get to Asher. Each strike was to head, neck, or heart. Men died before they hit the ground.

Back at the table, Asher had settled into a deep stance. He had lost his sword, somehow, possibly in one of the fallen bodies around him.

Instead, he wielded a chair in his right hand, using it either to bash at heads and legs, or using it as a cover to hide the motion of his dagger, which darted out, drawing blood.

This was where Asher truly shone. He was above average in every skill that made for a good warrior, but you could find others that had an edge over him. However, when things got violent and all plans fell to dust, that's where Asher ruled in chaos. This was one thing he'd never been able to teach his men.

He'd tried, of course. He'd had them train with one hand tied, or with an eye covered. Once, he even tied strings to their little fingers, running them down and tying them to their feet. The string would only pull tight if they raised their hands above their heads. Then he made them spar with each other as he stood by and threw rocks at them.

All of his squad had shown quick thinking and adaptability, most figured out most of the challenges, even if it took a little while. The problem was that, as they thought through the problem, they'd slow down. It was as if their brains could power problem-solving or a keen killer instinct, but not both.

For Asher, it was as natural as breathing. If anything, his bloodlust surged as things got complicated. He didn't have to look to know that the chair leg that just broke had a jagged point to it. He didn't need to adjust his footing to counter the man coming at him from behind. No, he just knelt, picked up the splintered chair leg and thrust it backward, catching the man just above the belt. Then he spun out of the way as the injured man fell forward, unable to stop his momentum, dropping his weapon as both hands jumped to the messy wound in his stomach.

Asher finished the man with a quick strike, then he was backpedaling furiously as three more converged. Like men gathering into a line, as they all headed toward him, they moved closer to each other. This created a perfect target for Mendar, who was running up behind the three.

Two quick slashes across backs had the two men in the rear screaming and twisting, trying to face this new attacker. The attacker in front also twisted, distracted by the thought of an attack from behind. That distraction was more than enough for Asher to reverse direction, close the distance, and plunge his dagger into the indecisive man.

"Stop! Stop! Stop!" A man was shouting and coming down a set of stairs that led to an office on the second level of the warehouse. He held his hands open above him, showing that he was unarmed. Asher kicked a dying man away and turned towards this fresh meat.

"Asher, stop!" The man shouted. Hearing his name gave Asher a moment of pause, but not much. It only served to show that the Tribulus was onto them. "I have a message for you!"

This brought Asher up short. The man came down the stairs and stopped, recoiling in horror at the bloodbath around him.

"What have you done?" The man quivered. "We are not your enemies. We've been waiting for you."

Asher laughed, throwing his head back and letting the sound wash the room. Some warriors would roar to celebrate a victory. Asher always laughed.

"Rabbits are always waiting for the wolf, friend,

they just don't know it." Asher's blood was pumping and he felt immortal. "If you knew it was me who had taken your tax collector, you should have prepared better."

"Collector?" the man stammered, trying to understand. "What do you mean? Every core station has your description and a standing invitation to deliver to you should you ever come to us. Who did you capture?"

Mendar cringed and looked towards Asher, who growled deep back in his throat. Here was proof that it was one of his own men running the Tribulus. For the first time, Mendar himself began to doubt.

"Why would I accept an invitation to such an obvious trap?" Asher began walking again, closing in on the messenger, who suddenly realized his position.

"The boss, the leader," he stammered. "He sent me a code word, just yesterday. He said you would understand."

As Asher closed on him, the man's voice turned pleading.

"What is the name of this boss?" Asher now stood in front of the man, dagger pointed at his stomach. "Tell me this code word you think will save you."

"Oh, please, no!" The man backed up a step, but hit the wall behind him. "I don't know his name. I've only met him once. He has his own crew that he uses to manage centers like mine."

The man's eyes flitted to Mendar, who was standing close.

"I was told to only say the code word to you."

Asher pressed the tip of his dagger into the man's stomach, enough to hurt, but not enough to draw blood.

"You have new instructions. Spit it out now. You've got me curious."

"Ander." The man gasped, short of breath from trying to pull his stomach in, away from the blade. "He said the code word was Ander!"

Asher froze.

He pulled back the dagger. Mendar looked at him and raised an eyebrow, but Asher wasn't offering any explanations.

"If I were to accept this invitation, where am I supposed to go?"

The man raised quivering hands and motioned one back towards his office.

"I have a map for you. It's on my desk."

Asher stood back.

"Mendar! Go with the man and retrieve this map of his."

Asher turned towards the back door where Tormand and Largan had entered, having heard Asher's laugh and knowing the battle was over. He beckoned to Tormand, who hurried over.

"Go with them." Asher ordered. "Mendar, Largan, and I are going to check out our next lead. You stay here with this man. Find out what he knows."

"Anything in particular?" Tormand asked.

"No," Asher answered. "Get everything. Wring him dry."

Tormand's smile was a vicious thing as he climbed the stairs, passing Mendar as he came back down.

"Let's go," Asher commanded, waving to Largan as well. Mendar looked back once at Tormand entering the office, shook his head, then followed Asher.

Chapter 17

"Go get Asher. He should be here."

Chapter 18

Asher stalked through the streets, Mendar and Largan at either hand, neither of them daring to speak. For all his skill in violence, Asher was seldom truly angry. He was angry now.

Beyond the implied betrayal of one of his old squad, there was also the revelation that the Tribulus knew where he had hid Eliana. If they imagined it would make Asher back off, they had sorely misjudged him. Now that there was an active threat, he would kill and keep killing until the threat was gone. It was all he knew.

They found the house on the map. It was appallingly normal, a near replica of the two houses on either side and across the street. It was a simple construction pattern that had caught on, nearly any man could build it, so most did.

"Are you sure this is the place?" Asher asked. Mendar was already double-checking the map.

"This is it. Do we knock? Should we scout the area first?"

Asher rounded on his two men.

"First, there's something we need sorted. If I go in

there and find one of our own men, I'm killing him. Do either of you have any problem with that?"

"No" Largan said immediately.

Mendar hesitated. That was answer enough.

"Largan, you're with me. Mendar, scout the area."

"Wait!" Mendar suddenly realized he was going to be shut out, sent away from Asher's side. It felt like something was being stolen from him. "I won't interfere."

"Not good enough," Asher snapped. "Besides, we really do need the area scouted. Do you really think Largan is capable of doing a thorough job on his own?"

"Hey!" objected Largan, though both of the other men ignored him. Mendar shook his head. It hurt to feel like he was being sent away, right at the most crucial moment, but the thinking part of his brain was still yelling that this was a trap.

Asher wasn't going to stop now, his anger was up and he'd run right into the trap. It wasn't that he was naive, he just believed that he could fight free of any trap, as he had in the past.

Mendar wasn't so sure. If men tried to jump him inside the house, Asher would be more than a match for them. The man excelled in closed spaces. So, if the trap were really dangerous, it would likely come from the outside. Mendar realized he probably only had minutes to scout around and find any hidden squads ready to pounce.

He nodded, accepting Asher's order, and left them, moving to the side of the house. As soon as he was out of sight, he increased his pace to a fast jog.

He didn't have much time.

Asher motioned Largan towards the front door.

"Kick it down," he ordered. Largan nodded and complied, taking three quick steps before launching a stomping kick into the door, just above the latch. Wood splintered and the door fell inwards. Asher walked in, sword and dagger at the ready.

"Master Asher!" A man exclaimed from the far end of the room. He had been sitting in a large chair facing the door. He stood now, arms wide in welcome. He didn't approach Asher, however, and three guards stood at attention a few yards in front of the man, effectively dividing the room in half.

Asher searched the man's face, and while it did seem familiar, it wasn't one of his old squad.

The man froze as Asher made no greeting in return, only searching the three guards, readying his next attack.

"It's me!" The man tilted his head towards the lamp, as if Asher couldn't see him. "Raca! Your prized pupil."

Asher turned to Largan, who nodded.

"I remember him. He was an excellent hand with the sword, but he failed the scar test. You sent him away."

"Failed?" The man's arms dropped, as did his expression. "I didn't fail, you whipped puppy. I thought I did, at first. Why, there was even a month or so when I considered killing you. But then I realized the true test."

"True test?" Asher raised an eyebrow.

"Of course!" the man crowed. "Being sent away was the true final test! Your squad were your subordinates, men who would follow your orders, die for you. I realized I wasn't that. But you didn't only want soldiers, did you? You wanted another man like yourself. Someone who could see things others did not. Somebody who understood the uses of fear and power."

He looked to Largan.

"Asher wouldn't want mindless dogs. No, he would want men who could think for themselves. What would it prove if I held still while he beat me? He sent me out to prove myself, to see what I would do without his orders. And look what I have done! I have built an empire, my captain. I have taken your lessons on fear and perfected them. King Stephan himself fears to move against me. Look at me now. What say you?"

"I remember you now," Asher mused. "You tried to fight back when you had promised to stand your ground. You squealed like a child when the blade touched your skin. I do seem to remember you had some talent with the blade, but you crumbled when

110

hit."

"Some talent?" The man took another step forward, his fists clenching. The facade of the eager pupil crumbled into bitterness. "I was your equal or better back then, and I have only grown better. You have other skills, it's true, but I have gained those as well and added more.

"I kept track of you throughout the war and ever since. You go through so much trouble to stand out, so people see the great Asher, the Laughing Killer. It also makes you absurdly easy to track. Did you think you were being clever, hiding your wife with the farmer?"

Asher tensed, his knuckles turning white on the handle of his sword.

"If you so much as laid a finger on..."

Raca waved his hand dismissively.

"I didn't harm your precious Eliana, though I'm surprised you haven't taught her to keep her mouth shut."

From beside him, Asher heard Largan's teeth grind against each other as his jaw clenched. He hadn't even met Eliana, but among the squad, she was regarded as something close to a distant goddess.

Raca clenched and unclenched his fists, seething. Largan could see the conflict in his eyes and suddenly understood the man. Largan's own father had been a drunkard, and had beaten Largan and his brothers when the liquor took hold. Largan hated his father. He had also craved the man's approval until the day he died. He saw the same thing in Raca now.

He hadn't actually believed that there was some final test, but he had hoped deeply that it was true. Even now, facing Asher's contempt, he wanted to kill his captain almost as much as he wanted to hear a word of respect.

"Why can't you see?" Raca raved. "Has farming filled your mind with dirt clods? You are the Tribulus. It was built for you. I greet you now as an equal. We are the same!"

Chapter 19

"The same?" Asher smiled, but there was no warmth in it. Something deep and primal within himself had awoken. "You compare yourself to me?"

The man started to speak and Asher cut him off.

"You have scared fat shopkeepers and farmers. You have ordered swaggering buffoons out onto safe streets to bully people. You think this makes you a big man? You think this makes you like me?

"I have haunted the dreams of warriors. I have crept among the spears and plucked the life from men who could shred through your whole organization in a day. I have harvested the very souls of hardened killers, staring in their eyes as it happened, just so they'd know I'd won.

"Same as me? SAME AS ME?" Asher seethed and roared through clenched teeth. "Child, you bark and the sheep scatter. I whisper and the wolves cower."

Asher trembled. He was ready to kill this man now. He held back for only a moment. There was a part of him that wanted to see Raca's reaction. He needed the man to know his place before Asher shredded through the three guards and cut his life's thread.

There was a long silence as Raca stared at Asher, his face as miserable as a wet cat. Asher drank in the sight.

"So, it really wasn't a test," he mumbled, more to himself than Asher. "You really couldn't see it. Then you're just another war-happy brute, aren't you?"

Asher tensed all over again. For one shining moment, the man had known Asher's disdain and had felt the weight of it. But he had bounced back quickly, too quickly.

It was time to end this.

"You claimed you were better than me at the blade," Asher taunted. "Care for a duel? It might save the lives of these guards."

Raca tilted his head, as if considering it.

"An amusing thought, but you already know I'm better than you, so you probably have some trick in mind. Your thrown dagger, perhaps? I'd rather you spend your last moments understanding that I am more cunning than you, as well."

With that, Raca stooped down and grabbed a rope that sat by his feet. He pulled and time seemed to move slowly as Asher followed the movement. The rope seemed to spring from the dirt as it broke free, traveling towards them. Its progress stopped suddenly as it snapped tight, the other end tied at the base of a pole to the right of Asher.

There was a moment's pause as the rope strained

and Asher's eyes flew up the pole.

"What in..." A large stone block perched above them, near the roof of the house. Ropes ran from it to each side, steadying it as its weight nestled on top of the single pole. Then Raca grunted with effort and the bottom of the pole slipped out. Asher sprang back, running into Largan on his left, getting clear of the falling block.

But Asher had misunderstood. The falling rock wasn't the trap, but rather the ropes attached to it. Each one was attached to part of the house's frame on their side of the house. As the massive weight hit the ends of the ropes, it jerked beams and supporting poles free.

Largan gripped Asher and threw him to the ground as the walls and roof fell down on them.

Chapter 20

Asher awoke to the sensation of burning in his lungs. He tried to draw a full breath and couldn't. He coughed and promptly inhaled enough dust to throw him into a fit of coughing. It was made exponentially worse by the fact that he couldn't breathe all the way. Every cough was a half-measure, and each breath only seemed to pump more dust and grit into his raw throat and lungs.

Something began to well up deep within him. He was trapped. Even as he coughed, he strained his muscles against the barrier he felt against his back. There wasn't even a whisper of a shift to the weight. Then he was thrashing, as best he could. What little motion he could manage was through wetness, and Asher could smell and taste blood.

The fear that had been building within him was erupting into a full panic.

His short, coughing breaths sharpened into a ragged panting. He tried to calm himself down, but the squeeze on his lungs made him dizzy. The sensation of feeling pinned in place like a bug under boot while the world spun was too much. Something within him snapped.

Asher screamed.

It was a short, gasping thing of a scream, but scream it was. And it was followed by another scream as Asher continued to thrash. Even as his mind tried to assert control over the panic that had gripped him, it only made things worse.

His arm touched a hand and he gripped it. The hand felt oddly cold and didn't grip back. It was also an odd angle. For their fingers to both be pointing the same way, as they were, the man would have to be on top of him.

Realization crashed down on him like another building. He was underneath Largan, and Largan wasn't moving.

Asher strained again, trying to pull his head back. But Largan's body had crushed around his. Asher's own head seemed to be indented into Largan's chest.

He pictured his own body crushed, mangled like Largan's.

He screamed again.

Each thought only made the fear worse as Asher screamed in a darkness he never could have imagined. He had spent his life around death, served it like a devoted son. He had never feared it, but he had always pictured his death coming on the battlefield.

His men believed that he never thought about such things, but he did. He had seen it too many times to not at least picture it for himself. He had prepared himself for the end, the sharp pain of a mortal wound fading as his blood abandoned him. His eyes would fade like all those others he had watched. Whatever it was that made him who he was would fade and disappear.

That is usually where Asher's musings stopped. He had never found much purpose in thinking about such things, though he suspected he knew more about souls than most priests. He had certainly seen enough of them leave dying bodies.

But now death seemed closer than ever before, and it wasn't the death Asher knew. This was a foreign death, a stranger. It seemed to claw at him, tempting him to let go, let the pain fade, the breath stop.

Asher's mind finally caught on a thought strong enough to counteract the panic.

Raca had beaten him.

The thought came to life like a struck match and helped burn away some of the black, choking panic around his heart. Anger started to breathe life back into him.

The little worm had set up a trap. He had talked about Asher being his idol, but in the end, he had a trap ready to spring. Asher had stepped right into it. Marauders had set hundreds of traps for him during the war, trying to catch or kill him like one of the beasts of the forest.

Back then, Asher had checked and double checked everything around him all the time. But now, he had turned soft. Months of regular farm work and quiet evenings with Eliana had dulled his instincts. And now that beetle of a man had crushed him under a building.

Asher felt the fire of anger burn brighter in his heart. He wasn't screaming anymore. A deep throaty growl rasped back and forth with each breath. He would survive. Oh yes, he would survive to kill Raca. He'd make it slow.

Asher fed on his daydreams of how he would kill Raca until the weight lifted from his chest to the sound of strained grunting and four strong hands gripped at his feet and waist and dragged him free.

A splinter of wood stabbed into the skin of Asher's ribs as he was drug over a beam, but it didn't matter. He was going to live.

He struggled to his feet, his mind bursting with relief to find that his legs still worked.

He could only imagine what he looked like. He blinked dirt out of his eyes and squinted at Mendar, who stared back at him in stunned silence.

The very ground seemed to sway under him and he gulped in deep breaths of air, hacking out dust from his lungs on every exhale. He reached out and gripped Mendar's shoulder, trying to hold himself upright. As his eyes focused, he began to see what was around him.

The front half of the building had fallen in, as Raca had planned, but it hadn't been clean. Falling beams had tilted against the rest of the house and more had fallen. A glowing fire was already spreading through the rest of the standing building. The oil lamp had fallen and broken. The fire was still small, still mostly fed by the oil, but once the timbers started to catch this whole area was going to go up in flames.

Asher looked closer and saw bits of cloth, as well as the odd hand or leg still under the wreckage. Raca had caught his own men in his trap and at least two of his guards were dead. There was no sign of Raca, though.

"Asher!" Mendar was trying to talk to him, but he couldn't quite get his thoughts in line yet. He glanced to the side and saw Largan's body. Mendar had pulled him out first, but there was clearly no saving the man.

Asher stumbled over to him, falling heavily to his knees and turned Largan's face towards him.

His skull was dented and his scalp was split. Blood soaked his face and shirt. He had absorbed most of the serious injuries Asher would have sustained, had Largan not thrown himself on top of him.

There was a flutter of eyelashes, and Asher thought he saw Largan's eyes focus on his face for a moment, but then the light behind the eyes were gone.

Largan was dead.

"Be at peace now," Mendar said behind him, a minuscule benediction for his fallen friend. But then Mendar was focused again on Asher.

"Asher!" Mendar repeated, while checking him over for wounds. He seemed incredibly insistent that Asher focus.

"Raca," Asher tried to say, but his throat was too ravaged by injury and grit to produce an actual tone. It came out as a haggard whisper. The attempt threw Asher into a coughing fit that made the world spin. He wasn't getting enough air to his lungs.

He pulled back from Mendar, though still kept a hand clamped on his shoulder for steadiness and looked around.

"Where?" he gasped, whispering the word as he searched the area.

"Asher!" Mendar yelled to counter Asher's whisper. "There was a man who stumbled away when I came back, but he's gone."

Asher gripped his shoulder even harder.

"Get him!" Asher tore at his throat, trying to growl the command. Mendar shook his head vigorously.

"Asher, we need to go now! Right now!" Mendar insisted, an odd hysterical note to his voice.

"I need to kill Raca." Asher gave up trying to match his tone to his emotions and whispered, finally producing intelligible words.

"No, you need to come back with me." Ander said.

Ander?

Asher turned and Ander was standing behind him. He scowled and his hand pawed at his waist, trying to find a dagger. His blades were gone, however, along with the belt. They had ripped free when Mendar pulled him from the building.

"You can't be here," Asher hissed a whisper at Ander, shocked that the honorable man would leave his post.

"Eliana is..." Ander's voice caught and he searched for something he could say. Then he steeled himself and delivered the news.

"Your wife is dying."

Chapter 21

Both men helped Asher walk as traumatized nerves tried to command bruised muscles. In the beginning, each man offered suggestions.

Maybe they should rest a moment?

Maybe over to that house for a drink of water?

They could steal that cart.

Asher dismissed every suggestion with an animal moan or growl, staggering forward with everything he had, panting and occasionally spitting blood. All that Ander and Mendar could do was hold his arms and keep him from toppling over whenever his foot hit a rock.

The more he moved, the more his head and lungs cleared. As soon as he could take a full breath without hacking, he no longer needed the support of the two men, though he still limped heavily on one side where a beam had struck the meat of his thigh, leaving a broad, painful bruise.

"I'm going to go on ahead," Ander said, once Asher didn't need his help to walk. Then he was gone, moving much fast than Asher could. Asher quivered at being left behind.

He moved faster and faster, ignoring the pain in his legs and his head. His lungs still burned, his raw throat and bruised ribs groaning at the exertion on his injured body, but he pressed for more speed.

Keeping Mendar close by, just in case, Asher finally broke into a steady jog, then a loping run, though he panted like a dog.

Fear drove him like a black creature, claws digging into his brain. His own pain was ignored, his injuries seen only as an annoyance, limiting his speed.

To Asher's mind, he ran for days, weeks, an eternity of pain before they finally stood outside Ander's snug cottage. Warm light glowed from the windows. The place looked so safe, secure, and happy. Asher hated it more than he had ever hated anything. The warm home had broken its promise of sanctuary.

Ander stood in front of the door, blocking their path.

"Get out of my way," Asher snarled, stalking forward. It was possibly the scariest he had ever looked. Blood he didn't remember bleeding mixed with tears he didn't remember crying and created a muddy mask that would have frightened any demon of the abyss.

"She's not in there." Ander's calm, firm voice was a more effective wall than his body. Asher felt himself breaking. Suddenly, his knees were loosening, the strength leaking away from his legs. He felt himself losing his balance, though now it had nothing to do with injured lungs or any physical pain.

"Where is she?" The snarl was gone. A hoarse, pleading whisper asked Ander one more time for hope he couldn't give.

"She has moved on."

Ander stepped forward quickly as Asher lost the last strength in his knees, catching him as he started to collapse. Asher clung to him, gripping tightly to his shoulders as the tears came, strong and hard. Asher buried his face into Ander's chest and wept like a child.

Chapter 22

"Who's fault is it?" Asher whispered, when the sobs had lessened.

Mendar felt a chill through his spine. He had seen Asher in full glory, a god of violence, but he shuddered to even consider what would happen to anyone Ander named at that moment.

"No one is at fault," Ander assured him firmly. "Her labor started far too early. Her body wasn't prepared. Rachel thinks some other sickness stressed her body. There is nothing that could have been done differently. We all hate the fact, but these things happen. Every woman who brings a child into this world faces down death, as sure as any soldier on the battlefield."

Asher had found strength in his legs again and now stood. His head was still bowed and his shoulders rose and fell with each heavy breath.

"Whose fault is it?" he repeated. Ander and Mendar could both hear the urgency in his voice. Asher had never felt grief like this. This was a new pain, one he had never known, delivered in a level beyond comprehension. He had no way to process it, so he turned to the only thing he knew: violence. Something had been taken from him, and now Asher needed revenge.

"Was it my fault?" Asher asked, his voice even more urgent. "Was this because of something I did? Is this punishment for who I am? If this was my fault, I swear I'll kill..."

Ander slapped him. The full weight of the farmer's arm, strengthened by years working with dirt, water, and stone, rocked Asher's head hard to the side. Mendar took half a step forward, but what was he going to do?

Ander wasn't done. He hit Asher over and over, knocking his body side to side. Never did he hit with a closed fist, each strike was open-handed, meant to sting, to inflict pain instead of injury.

Asher's fingers hung limply at his sides. Never once did they raise to defend himself. Never once did they search for his missing daggers. Mendar understood all at once.

Ander had somehow understood. Asher had no way to process emotional pain, but needed to feel something. In this bizarre spectacle, Ander was helping Asher connect with his grief through physical pain. Mendar was horrified by the spectacle.

Finally, Asher's head came up, annoyance and anger starting to rekindle in his eyes. This was what Ander had been waiting for.

He stopped. Asher stood once again on his own

two feet, a more familiar snarl on his face, though there was still something manic flitting about his eyes.

Then a new thought occurred to him.

"Where is she?" Asher whispered the question. Ander shifted his feet.

"She's in there," he answered simply. He knew that grief did strange things to a man. "But Asher, you know she's..."

"Where is she?" Asher sprung at Ander, swatting away the hands that raised to defend himself. It was as if the weakness and injuries were suddenly gone, washed away by some new, overwhelming need.

Ander's eyes widened as Asher gripped his throat with bloody fingers. He didn't grip, but his fingers felt like cold steel.

Asher's eyes were wild, but still intensely focused on the farmer.

"I know her body is in there. I know it is dead. But that isn't her. I've killed enough men to know that something leaves them. Whatever that is left her, but it has to go somewhere. So where is she?"
Asher's eyes didn't leave Ander's for a moment. He wasn't even blinking.

"Well, different people believe..."

Asher struck him, hard, with the flat of his hand. Ander's head rolled to the side and stars filled his vision, but it cleared quickly as Asher shook him.

"Where is she?" The question was hissed through

clenched teeth. Asher's eyes were increasingly bloodshot, but no tear escaped his eyes.

"You can't just..." Ander started.

Asher hit him again.

"Tell me where she is. You and your freak son know more than you should. You're more calm than you should be. So, tell me what you know."

Ander straightened his knees under him, which had been feeling a little loose.

"I worship the Old God," he stated firmly. He understood now that Asher needed a firm hand. For all his physical force, the man was on the verge of mental collapse, if that moment hadn't already come and gone.

Asher nodded. His prisoner had started to divulge real information, he could feel it and responded to it.

"I do not know this god," Asher started, then waved Ander to silence when he started to offer more information. "Nor do I care to. It is enough for me that you know. Where is my wife? Is she with this god?"

"Not yet." Ander spoke firmly, with all the authority of a man confident in his faith. "The souls of the departed linger until the last of their loved ones have passed on as well."

Suddenly, Asher's eyes were brimming with tears. They streamed through the dirt on his face as he tried to choke out his next question.

"She's... She is... waiting for me?"

"Yes."

"And she is here?" Asher sniffed. His jaw quivered. Ander drew him in, holding the quaking man.

"Close your eyes," Ander commanded. It was an unnecessary order, as Asher's face was now pressed tightly into Ander's shoulder.

Asher nodded as best he could as another silent sob shook his body.

"Now, think about Eliana. Try to focus on her purest form. Forget how she looked, how she sounded, everything about what she left behind. Try to think about what you felt when she was near."

Another nod.

"Can you feel it now? She would be close at such a time."

A long silence followed. Ander offered no more guidance.

Finally, Asher straightened, his eyes dry and cold.

"Thank you," he whispered. Then, somehow straightening even more, he spoke in a leveled, controlled tone. "I appreciate your family's attention to my wife in her final hours. Please dispose of the body, she no longer needs it.

"Mendar, come!" Asher snapped, turning on his heel and striding away, only a shadow of a limp remaining.

Mendar hurried to catch up, but did not actually walk next to Asher. He knew Asher better than anyone, but even a stranger would have known to steer clear of the thundercloud that was Asher on that long walk.

Chapter 23

They were back in the city before Mendar had thought of a single thing to say. He had about decided to ask Asher what their next move was when they were interrupted.

A man lurched out at them from an alley. Mendar had his sword out and pointed at the man before he had made it two steps, but attack wasn't what the man had in mind.

It was the man who had come into the tavern the day before. Even had his face not been familiar, the distinctive limp would have given him away.

"Please!" The man raised both hands in front of him. It was desperation that drove the man, not violence. Mendar lowered his sword, though didn't sheath it. "I'm willing to pay. I have no one left to help me."

The man held out a small pouch and shook it, a dull clink of coins came from within. To Mendar's amazement, Asher turned and reached out his hand, accepting the small bag, which he tossed to Mendar.

"Lead on, sir."

"Asher!" Mendar scolded. "You are in no shape to

do anything tonight!"

Asher waved him away and followed the limping man into the darkness.

Mendar tried to see the angle as the two of them followed after the man. While they walked, the man babbled gratitude while he gave them the details.

The man's name was Deacon. His daughter had fallen in love with a man and married him. She had moved into the man's family home, where he lived with three of his brothers who helped work the farm. During the first year, the father had seen her less and less. The last time he had seen her, she had a scar across the back of her arm and she wouldn't meet his eyes, only asked him to leave.

"I went back there to confront the man. His brother met me on the porch and knocked me to the ground. They threatened to kill me if I came back.

"I went to the guard, but they told me that a man is free to do what he likes on his own land. I could not deny that she had married him of her own free will. But the law acts as if he owns her! I sit and think about her slaving away for those four brutes and I want to tear them to shreds!"

Deacon had worked himself into a full lather. He was spitting the words now. His limp was even more pronounced as he tried to hurry, but only succeeded in stumbling more.

"But I can't." Mendar could practically hear the man's teeth grind as he clenched his jaw in frustration at his injured leg. After a few moments, he shook his head, as if clearing it. "But if you come talk to them, I think they'd let her go. A couple of the brothers served in the army. They've heard about you, admire you. So, if anyone could get them to listen, it would be you. I only want her home again."

"I'm not going to talk to them." Asher spoke for the first time since leaving the cabin in the woods. He did not explain further, even when Deacon was foolish enough to ask.

"Is that the house?" Asher's voice was dangerously void of any emotion. Mendar looked over at his captain and hoped there would be something on the other side of his grief.

"Yes!" The limping man nodded enthusiastically and gestured at the darkening sky. "They'll all be home now."

"Perfect." Asher strode towards the house. "Stay there."

Mendar hesitated. Had he meant both of them, or only Deacon?

"Captain!" he hissed, holding out his sword. "Take this!"

Asher acted as if he hadn't heard the offer and continued walking towards the house. Mendar churned for a moment, wondering if he should stay behind, as ordered, or follow his captain. He didn't want to anger Asher, but he was acting very strangely.

He compromised and followed at a distance, first ordering the older man to stay hidden. So it was that Mendar was a good thirty paces behind Asher when he came to the door of the house. The whole dwelling was a squalid affair sprawling over a wide area. The family had built on to the building as they needed more space, but never bothered to improve the existing structure. As a craftsman, Mendar was offended by the slipshod way the place had been thrown together. It all worked, of course, the house stood, but there wasn't a single square corner or level beam. They had relied heavily on daubing mud to fill the holes in the walls, rather than actually craft the logs to fit together well.

Mendar jumped as Asher paused only for a moment before sending a jarring kick into the front door. The lazily-mounted door broke on one hinge, but then hung by the remaining joint and the latch, twisting diagonally, rather than breaking down into the house.

This seemed to enrage Asher and he kicked and stomped at the remaining hinge until it too broke free and the door toppled sideways, partially blocking the door.

By now, four shouting brothers were already pushing from the other side, trying to get out at this wild man who had kicked their door down.

Asher leapt over the wreckage of the door and slammed into the group, sending a jarring punch into the first one's neck. The man stumbled back, gasping and choking. Then the other three were on Asher, pulling him in and piling on punches and kicks of their own.

Mendar swore bitterly and sprinted forward to jump into the fray. Asher didn't even have a weapon. The captain could easily have used the narrow passage of the doorway to funnel the four brothers, make them come at him one at a time, at least until someone thought to go out the back door and run around. That is what Mendar had been waiting for, but now Asher was already several seconds into a fight that would likely last less than a minute.

Mendar drew his sword as he ran and used the point to push the biggest brother back. He fit the description Deacon had given of his daughter's husband. It was a restrained move, it would draw only a couple drops of blood at most. Mendar wasn't completely on board with the idea of killing the four men. There was no need to escalate the situation.

The sword point did its job and the biggest brother backed off enough for Mendar to reach down with his free hand and yank Asher back to his feet.

Asher, however, came off the ground with a spike of splintery wood from the broken door in his hand. He drove it hard into the thigh of his nearest opponent, then ripped himself free from Mendar's grip to fling himself at the husband, who was still standing back slightly at the tip of Mendar's sword.

A cut above Asher's eye spilled blood down his face, adding to Largan's dried blood that was still caked on his face. Asher's target tried to take a step back, away from the savage creature leaping at his face, but he tripped and went down. Asher landed on top of him and started pounding away at the man's ribs, trying to break them.

Mendar intercepted the remaining uninjured brother, looping an arm around his neck and pulling him backwards, off balance.

The brute that Asher had punched in the throat, while still wheezing and sucking for breath, grabbed up a wooden chair and flung it at Asher's back, knocking him off and dealing a significant blow to his head.

The brother with the spike in his leg, seeing the tactic succeed, grabbed another chair and threw it, hitting Asher again.

The big one on the floor held one arm tight to his ribs, but he was coming off the floor.

And Asher wasn't.

His eyes were still open, but they were unfocused and bleary. More blood flowed down his neck from a new wound on his head. Head wounds always bled freely.

The man Mendar was holding twisted and threw an elbow back into his gut. Air rushed out of him and he felt his knees weaken. He managed to keep his arm around the man's neck, but only barely. One more strike like that and he would rip free. Then Mendar would have his hands too full to save Asher. The man on the ground was already up on one knee and was drawing out a hunting knife from his boot, looking at Asher with pure rage. It was about to end.

Enough.

Chapter 24

Mendar lowered his arm enough to admit the edge of his sword, which he drew quickly across his captive's neck.

The brother with the injured throat saw it happen and gave a choked cry. Then Mendar was across the room and leveled a kick at the daughter's husband as he raised over Asher with his hunting knife, striking him in the head and sending his knife bounding across the packed earth floor.

Then he turned and struck down the brother with the spike in the leg, who had been limping towards another chair to throw. The last one, still clutching at his throat, looked with horror at the devastation , his brothers suddenly gone in a few moments of focused violence. Mendar chopped him down like a young sapling.

Mendar stood panting amongst the devastation. The brothers were either dead or on their way. He didn't know how serious the injuries were on the husband, but he had no intention of checking. Mendar didn't care. He'd already made a decision about this house and everything in it.

He lifted Asher to his feet. The man was barely coherent, but he could walk with assistance.

As he guided his captain through the ruined door, he heard a whimper. He turned and saw Deacon's daughter, huddled in the corner, one hand over her mouth. Her eyes widened when she realized she had been seen.

Her clothes were filthy and her hair hung in strands. She might have been pretty once, but hard living had made her haggard.

"Are you going to kill me?" she whimpered.

"No, but I am going to burn this house to the ground. I advise you to go find whatever family you might have left."

He saw no reason to tell her that her own father had ordered this, even if the man hadn't known what he was unleashing. For that matter, Mendar himself had been unprepared for Asher's recklessness.

The woman sobbed and fled out the back door. Mendar took an oil lantern from where it hung on the wall and flung it on the broken door as he helped Asher out. The broken wood made for the perfect makings of a fire and soon the whole shack was ablaze.

Mendar made no attempt to talk to Deacon or his daughter. The job was done and thoroughly. The two would make their own way from here. He heard Deacon call her name as he guided Asher into the night.

By the time they were halfway back to the inn, Asher was walking without assistance, though he still looked pale from blood loss. Mendar pulled them into the first tavern they came to and pulled Asher to a deserted table. He shot a look at an approaching waitress that sent her scampering back where she came from. He saw her whispering to the innkeeper, who shook his head at her. It was enough, they wouldn't be disturbed.

"Care to explain yourself?" Mendar growled. Asher looked up at him, his eyes barely focused and surprisingly, full of tears. One rolled down Asher's cheek as he shrugged.

"Those were bad men and they hurt that girl. Now they're dead and the world is better for it. What's your problem?"

"Whether or not they deserved to die is a discussion for another time. Personally, I think a good beating would have done the job nicely. But I'm talking about your approach. You didn't think, you didn't plan. You literally jumped in, fists swinging. For all that is holy, you didn't even have a stance!"

Mendar quivered in rage, but Asher absorbed it all without a flicker of emotion or response.

"You backed me into a corner where I had to kill those men. They weren't even Tribulus. They were just dumb brutes. You owe me an explanation, Asher. I've followed you through every kind of nightmare I could have imagined and more, but I've also always trusted you to get us through. I've seen everything from you except stupidity, which was here in spades tonight. Will you really say nothing?"

Asher only stared, a pale statue. Mendar threw his hands in the air in frustration.

"Are you trying to get yourself killed?"

A blink and Asher looked away and down. The awkward moment stretched on as Mendar's anger bled away from him.

"That's it, isn't it? You weren't trying to win. You certainly didn't care about that poor girl. You were looking for a way out. That's something else I've never seen from you, Asher: cowardice."

Asher's head jerked up and a little flame finally showed behind his bloodshot eyes. Mendar followed it and piled on.

"Do you think you'll see Eliana again? Do you think she's watching you? Well, then consider the moment when you see her again. Do you really want to have her look at you in shame? Her great husband, the mighty Asher, flailing about and getting himself killed because he felt sorry for himself. I can barely stand to look at you. What makes you think she'd want to spend another second with you?"

Asher growled and slammed his fist on the table, the blood on his face and his red eyes making for a truly terrifying sight, but Mendar still pushed.

He knew there would be a decision made tonight.

There had to be.

Asher was at a crossroads and Mendar knew it. Before him was a broken mind, there was no going back to how it was before. The best he could hope for was that it would reform into something stable. If it stayed broken, Asher wouldn't live out the year.

So Mendar pushed.

"Look at yourself. You're pathetic. If you want to join Eliana, that's fine, but do it in a way that'll let you hold your head up when you see her again. If you do anything less than your best, either she'll know and think you a coward, or she'll believe that it really was the best you could do. So, which is it? Would you rather she see you as cowardly or weak?"

Asher held his head with both hands, as if trying to hold it together.

"She can see me," he whispered.

"Then be a good man!" Mendar shot back. Asher looked up, genuine fear in his eyes.

"I don't think I can. I'm not like you."

"You kill evil people. That's a good thing." Mendar knew it was a stretch, but they were deep into it now.

Asher stared back at him for a protracted amount of time.

"It's good to kill evil people." Asher said the words and Mendar felt a ping of concern. He hadn't meant it exactly like that.

Asher's chair fell backwards as he leapt to his feet. He quickly put a hand on the table to steady himself. Standing quickly after a head wound didn't have the intimidating effect Asher had likely been hoping for.

Mendar stood with him, accepting whatever challenge Asher had to offer. It wouldn't be much. In his current state, Asher was no match for Mendar, but Mendar had already accepted that Asher might require more violence to process his emotions. It might even cost their friendship.

Asher joined his second hand to the one on the table and stood, hunched over and shaking while Mendar waited for him to make a move, any move.

Finally, Asher looked up and his eyes were calm. There was still a deadness behind them that worried Mendar, but the frantic madness was gone.

"You're a good man, Mendar."

"Thank you?" Mendar couldn't keep the puzzlement from his voice. He hadn't been prepared for the statement. It wasn't spoken as a compliment, more as an observation, or possibly, as a sentence passed upon him.

"Come with me. There's something that needs to be done."

Mendar shook his head.

"We're not going anywhere but back to the inn. You can barely stand. You need rest."

"We're going to the inn," Asher replied.

"Oh, ok." Mendar didn't recognize the tone in his mentor's voice. He had said a normal thing, but he'd made it sound like a dark pronouncement.

144

Chapter 25

The trip back to the inn was made in silence. When they came in, the innkeeper and Tormand leapt to their feet.

"You're all right!" Tormand crowed. "I was telling fatso here that it would take more than a collapsed building to stop the Laughing Killer."

Asher stared at Tormand.

"You're a bad person, aren't you?"

Tormand flashed his signature grin, a wild thing.

"I'm no angel, I'll admit it." He shrugged.

"You enjoy hurting people," Asher continued. "You hold back from a fear of consequences, but if given free rein, you would hurt a lot of people, wouldn't you?"

"Where is all this coming from?" Tormand questioned, stepping towards Asher. "How hard did you get hit on the head? You've always said I enjoyed my work, but I learned from you. Remember that time–"

Asher took two steps and slammed his fist up into Tormand's chest from below. It happened so fast that none of them had time to process that Asher had lifted Mendar's dagger from his belt. The two men stood like statues. Asher was braced, as if holding Tormand up. Tormand tensed around the blade now nestled underneath his ribs. He moved as if to cough, but his lungs didn't work how they should.

The strength drained from him and he sagged against the knife in Asher's hand. Asher crouched, lowering himself to the ground with Tormand, finally laying the dead soldier flat on the ground. His life gone, Tormand was limp as a rag.

Asher rose to petrified silence from Mendar and the innkeeper.

Asher turned the bloody knife towards the innkeeper.

"Are you a good person or a bad person?" he asked. The innkeeper started to babble, and Asher interrupted him. "Do not dare lie in this moment. This might be the most important moment of your life. So tell me, are you a good person or a bad person."

The innkeeper gulped, his eyes flicking first towards Tormand's body on the floor, then to Mendar, still standing by the door. He found no help or inspiration from either source.

"I... I suppose I'm neither. That is to say, I think I still have bits of both in me. I am a lazy man, and a glutton, but I don't cheat my customers and I keep my word."

Asher waited a moment, keeping Mendar's dagger pointed at the man. Then, a decision was reached, and he lowered the blade. He spoke nothing more to the innkeeper, but instead turned to Mendar.

"We no longer have any deals or compromises with evil men. We kill them. Is that understood?"

Mendar nodded, dumbly, wondering in the back of his mind how much of this was his own doing.

"Men like this," he gestured towards the innkeeper, "we leave alone or allow them to help us. We cannot try to hunt down every flawed human being."

"How do we decide who is evil?" Mendar asked, carefully. It was hard to know how sane Asher was at that moment. To his surprise, Asher shrugged.

"I hope I'll know it when I see it. For now, we have plenty on our plate with the Tribulus. Anyone who would steal a child for personal gain is evil. Anyone who would support them is evil. That's all we need for now."

Asher sat down heavily and called for food, which the innkeeper was quick to bring. He polished off most of a roast and half a loaf of bread. Then he got started on some venison stew. It was enough food for three men, but Mendar had seen this before with injured men. The body, in desperate need of repair, craved all the food it could get. And as expected, as soon as he was done, Asher excused himself and fell asleep.

Mendar took a moment to breathe. He hadn't had a chance to feel much of anything, himself. Getting

Asher through the last twelve hours had been an absolute ordeal. Now, the deaths that had stacked up during the day came crashing down on Mendar's psyche.

Eliana was dead.

Largan was dead.

Tormand was dead.

He hadn't even liked Tormand, but his death was so sudden. It had also been a chilling brand of violence. While Mendar certainly couldn't argue that Tormand was a bad person, it still sat poorly with him that Asher had murdered the man so casually. Tormand had served with Asher nearly as long as Mendar himself.

Even the fact that Asher was sleeping right that moment seemed oddly disrespectful to the dead.

And then there was this new directive. Mendar had signed on to exterminate the Tribulus. While he had been scared about what it would mean if they lost, he had still felt good about what they were doing. The Tribulus had become a major issue. And if anyone could outmatch them, it was Asher.

But now it sounded like Asher was going to continue his rampage, even after the Tribulus was gone. Mendar reached out for his cup and was surprised to see that his hand was shaking.

What had he gotten himself into?

Chapter 26

In spite of his injuries, Asher arose before Mendar and the innkeeper and headed out onto the street, hobbling from stiff muscles and joints. He hadn't slept as peacefully as Mendar had assumed.

The colors of the world had changed. Everything was a little darker, a little grayer, and there was a large part of his mind that welcomed it. A world without his wife deserved to be darker for it.

But he also realized that he no longer fit in the world, not the way he was. It felt like he didn't belong in his own skin. The very fineness of his clothes offended him. The colors that once drew attention now seemed tasteless and garish.

He didn't even notice the stares from the people around him. He hadn't bothered to clean himself before leaving the inn. His hair hung in bedraggled clumps, old blood binding them together. Brown flecks of dried blood also covered his face like some sort of skin disease. Everyone hurried to get out of his way, but he didn't see them.

His mind was more focused than he had ever remembered. It was as if he could only think one thought at a time. Gone were the distractions of a flitting mind. Instead, he was a still pool within. Right now, the thought that dominated his mind was that he was losing. His conscious mind knew that the Tribulus was only responsible for one of the deaths the day before, but on a deeper level, he felt his own side shrinking as the opposing side grew stronger.

It couldn't happen. He couldn't lose, not after all he had already lost.

But he couldn't see the path forward. So, he needed someone who knew more than he did. He needed someone who knew secrets.

He found her by her hovel. It was an abandoned shed outside a house that had largely fallen in on itself. Ironically, the shed had been made more sturdily than the house, so that is where Baba had made her home. As far as Asher was aware, he was the only one who knew about it.

She sat on her haunches, crouching over a tiny cook fire, heating some kind of soup, from the looks of it.

"Well, if it isn't..." She started a lazy drawl, her attention still on her meal, but she stopped abruptly when she lifted her head and saw him. "Good heavens, boy! What happened to you?"

In her moment of true surprise, she sat up ramrod-straight and spoke without the old-woman waver in her voice.

"Eliana is dead."

Baba gasped, her hand to her mouth.

"Oh, dear Asher, I'm so, so sorry. Was it... was it them?" She held her hand to her mouth, as if trying to stop the words, but she was a woman defined by her curiosity, she simply could not resist the question and all the answer would mean.

Asher opened his mouth to speak, but found that the words wouldn't come. His body wasn't responding as it should. He shook his head, then wiped away a treacherous tear that had leaked from his eye.

"The child?" she prompted in a whisper. Asher shook his head again, and now her tears matched his own. She didn't move to hug him, neither were of that kind, but they shared a moment of profound sadness there in their silent tears.

Finally, Asher found his voice again.

"There was some complication with the birth. She didn't survive." He had intended a larger explanation, but finished quickly when he found his voice starting to betray him again.

"What now, then?" It was an abrupt question, but Baba understood better than most what was required in that moment. There were no words that could comfort Asher. What he needed now was direction. If left in his own mind, he would churn until he burned out.

Asher seized upon the question.

"The Tribulus. I need to finish the job. And then I

need to find anyone else like them. Baba, can you help me?"

She looked him up and down with a critical eye.

"Not with that hair, I can't."

"Loan me your knife, would you?"

She handed it to him, handle first.

"Be careful, it's sharp."

Asher gathered a thick fistful of hair, twisting it into a thick rope, then sawed through the entire mass right up close to the scalp. He held the matted locks in his fist in front of his face for a moment before dropping the mass to the floor. He then gathered another handful and repeated the procedure. Baba looked on impassively until every strand of Asher's beautiful long hair had been sliced free.

Chapter 27

The resulting mess of uneven scruff somehow transformed Asher's entire body. He looked pale now, and thin, like a starving animal. Still, the fire behind his eyes burned even brighter now, verging on madness, now without even a wisp of stray hair to temper the harshness of his gaze.

Baba whistled appreciatively.

"Now we're getting somewhere," she murmured. "Let me see if I can find you something to wear."

She rummaged around in her shed and came out with a moth-eaten shirt and a worn pair of shoes. The toes were no longer attached, which turned out to be good, as the things were too small for Asher's feet. His large toes poked out from the cracked leather.

Asher looked down at them and wiggled a toe, but offered no complaint, asked no questions.

Baba let him keep his pants, they looked rough enough from having been buried under a building and dragged back out. She finished her masterpiece with a smelly cloak that had once been wool.

"Anytime there are people around, clutch the cloak around you as if you're cold, no matter what temperature it is."

"So people will think I'm sick?" Asher guessed.

"Don't try too hard to make up people's minds for them." Baba warned. "Some will think you sick, some will think you mad, but all will avoid knowing more. That is the beauty of making other people uncomfortable. It's not even a conscious decision. Normal people avoid discomfort instinctively."

"I've got it. I make people uncomfortable, and they'll avoid me." Asher nodded along with this new education.

"That's true, but it's only half of the truth. 'Avoid you' makes it sound like a conscious decision. If you do it right, they won't even think about you. I believe that most people are basically good at heart."

Asher raised an eyebrow and she scowled at him, offended at his skepticism.

"Well, I do! What business is it of yours if I choose to believe in a little goodness in the world? The point is that a good person, if they think about it, will realize that, with enough effort, they could probably help you. They could pay for a good meal, a room, fetch a doctor, maybe let you stay in their home while you recover."

Asher scoffed.

"No one is going to do that!"

Baba smiled as if she had just won an argument.

"Exactly. It would be too much time and effort for too big of a risk. Still, if they thought about it, that's

154

the conclusion they would come to. And then they would be forced to decide not to help you, which would make them feel guilty. The simplest answer to this conundrum is to not think about it at all. No conclusion, no decision, no guilt."

"You're sure you believe that people are good? What you described makes people sound rather heartless."

"But they don't want to be! That's the point. There's too much wretchedness in the world for any good person to fix. They would destroy themselves and their families trying. So, rather than decide against trying, they don't think about it at all. Doesn't that make them good? An evil person could easily decide not to help. A good person will let their thoughts skip over people like us."

Asher ducked his head and scowled. On the one hand, he was fairly certain that what she had explained didn't make any sense. On the other hand, he couldn't seem to come up with any meaningful counterargument. He decided to stop trying.

"Fine, so if we make people uncomfortable, they won't see us. I can certainly see how that would be useful. Nobody looks at trash, like you said."

She raised an eyebrow.

"Is that what you thought I meant by that?" She cocked her head to the side, weighing his interpretation a moment before continuing. "Now you can at least move. With that hair and cloak, I'm surprised you could see anything, stomping around muddying the water all the time. Now let's make your pond a little bigger. How fast can you climb a wall? It's useful to be able to move up and down, as well as side-to-side."

Asher shrugged.

"I don't know how well I'd do at the moment, but generally I'd say I'm faster than most."

"Would you say you're faster than me?" An eager glint in her beady eyes made Asher pause.

"I would say that if I were, you wouldn't have asked me that question. Let's assume you're faster. Care to explain how? You can't pretend you're stronger than me."

"Strength matters less than the application of strength." Baba spoke as if quoting some holy writ. She smiled broadly, but Asher didn't get the joke. Her smile dimmed and she sighed, waving him to follow her. She led him around the back of her shed, which was a solid wall of stone, the seams so closely fitted that little mortar was used.

Asher ran his hands along the seams, then looked disbelievingly towards the fallen house.

"How is it that the house is a wreck, but the shed is built like a fort?" he asked. Baba shushed him.

"It's a sad story, and sad stories are a waste of time. There are too many of them for any single one to mean anything. You're here to learn. Climb the wall."

156

Asher sidled up to the wall and dug his fingers into the tiny gaps in between stones. The edges were rounded, so he held his body close to the wall, trying to get enough traction to lift his body from the ground. His toes, sticking out the end of his shoes, were able to find one good toehold near the bottom row of stones. He lifted himself off the ground, wincing a little as his bruised body objected to the strain. Then he started feeling over the stone for another handhold.

He found one, but when his hand slipped, everything came loose and he fell backwards, luckily only falling a foot or two, landing lightly.

Baba rolled her eyes at him, then approached the wall herself. She went up the side of the wall like a spider, her arms and legs moving lightly. Asher blinked. It didn't even look like her fingers were gripping the stone. It was more like a light touch. When she returned to the ground, she smiled a moment, enjoying his confusion.

Then she turned her hands palm up for him to inspect.

Iron hooks protruded out from under her sleeves, the hooked tips facing forward. Asher reached out and gave one a tentative tug. Baba's whole arm moved with the hook.

"They're strapped onto your arms?" Asher guessed. Baba nodded. "Isn't that uncomfortable? Any harness that would keep them that stable is going to chafe if you wear them all day."

"What did I tell you about discomfort?" Baba asked.

"You said people avoid it. Of course, they do."

"I said that normal people avoid it. You aren't normal and shouldn't try to be. I'll tell you the great secret all those normal people don't know, the secret that keeps them normal."

She leaned in as if there were anyone around who could hear them.

"Comfort is weakness. It's like the force of gravity itself. Everyone feels the need to be comfortable, but with every moment of comfort, your body weakens, your soul atrophies."

"Is that why you live in a slum?" Asher asked, barely keeping the sneer from his voice. "Do you really think it would hurt your soul to sleep in a bed with a solid roof over your head?"

"It wouldn't hurt me, no," she responded as if thinking through her words one by one. "But I would lose an opportunity to get stronger, sharper. Tell who is more focused than a hungry man. Tell me who is stronger than the blacksmith who spends all day moving heavy steel. If you want strength, then embrace discomfort. If you want to scale a wall fast enough that a guard won't see you in-between his rounds, then you'd better be ready to scrape off a fingernail or two and not whine about it.

"The bands I use to mount these hooks to my

arms once rubbed blisters. Now they sit firmly on leathery calluses. As you embrace discomfort, your body and mind will respond, making you stronger."

She cocked her head to the side for a moment, then added, "That being said, if you need an ointment, I have an assortment."

Asher stared after her as she hurried away, returning with a spare set of hooks. They were a little small, but it didn't take long to get them seated where they would sit easily in his palms. Now he approached the wall again. The iron points fit neatly into the gaps. The mortar scratched away easily any time he needed a better hold.

He experimented with looping the strap around the bottom of his elbow, so when the hook was set into the wall, he could use his elbow for leverage.

With his body still weak from blood loss, it was still an embarrassingly long time before he made it to the top of the shed, but as he sat there, catching his breath, something felt right again.

It had been a while since he had learned something new. He hadn't considered it, but he had been in a rut, playing it safe with what he already knew. Now, his mind stirred with new ideas. How fast could he get with these? What about the defensive capabilities? It was no small thing to have his arm lined with an iron bar. What if he could extend the hooks?

A small smile tugged at the corners of his mouth.

Chapter 28

Mendar paced the floor of the inn. Asher hadn't been back in a week. Each day, he expected him to burst through the door, or to hear some news about a bloody battle in the streets. But while both he and the innkeeper gathered all the news they could, nobody had heard anything about the Laughing Killer. Nobody had seen him.

Mendar was on the verge of pulling his hair out. He was already past the time when he had promised his wife he would be home, at least to check in. But what if Asher came back while he was gone? And rather than mopping up the last of the gang, as he thought they'd be doing, the Tribulus seemed stronger than ever. If he went home now, he might very well be leading them right to his family. He hadn't noticed anyone following him, but that wasn't a risk he felt he could take. After all, they had been following Asher.

Should he try to continue what his captain had started? Should he start investigating the Tribulus himself? Surely there were more people out there who knew something.

He sat down and considered his angles for an entire five seconds before rising again to pace.

"Enough, Mendar. You're making me dizzy."

Mendar spun at the voice from the door. A haggard figure stood there, dressed in black rags, his hair ragged and head down. There was something familiar about the figure, but something wasn't right. Were those Asher's boots?

A hand gripped Mendar's shoulder and a cold blade pressed against his throat. He froze, cursing himself.

"Not bad, eh?" a voice whispered in his ear. Then he was released and spun around.

There was Asher, the real Asher, though Mendar had to blink a couple times as his mind processed the new image his captain now wore. His full hair was gone, replaced by patchy tufts, mostly hidden under the cowl of a ragged cloak. His eyes were steady and focused, almost too focused, as they seemed to drill into Mendar's own.

"Where have you been?" Mendar exclaimed, while still studying this new Asher.

"I've been around town," Asher replied simply. "I've been researching the Tribulus."

"Oh, have you?" Mendar retorted. "Because we have also been 'around town' and we haven't seen you. We haven't even seen anyone who's seen you."

"Were they looking for this?" Asher spread his arms in his tattered cloak. Something at the back of

Mendar's mind nudged at him that Asher didn't seem to be wearing any blade, but he had definitely felt cold steel on his throat. This new Asher came with surprises.

"I suppose not," Mendar admitted. He glanced back at the other man who had been by the door, but that figure was already gone, disappearing back onto the street. He hadn't been searching among the bums and beggars. How many had he passed by? Had he seen Asher?

He looked at Asher anew, trying to remember. Asher smiled back at him, but it was a different smile now, one that didn't touch his eyes. Mendar shivered.

"Yes, I have seen you nearly every day for the past week, old friend."

"And you said nothing?" Mendar snapped, covering his uneasiness with anger. "We've been going out of our minds here. For all I knew, you were captured or killed by the Tribulus and my family was next! What were you thinking?"

"Your family is fine, I checked in on them earlier today."

That brought Mendar up short. He felt a little guilty for the thought, but one of the most surprising things was that Asher had thought to check on his family at all.

"For now, the Tribulus seem to think that I am dead. They have returned to business as usual. In fact, our innkeeper friend here should be expecting a

162

visit from collectors very soon."

The innkeeper paled.

"But I've been closed!" Vander exclaimed. "How am I supposed to pay them when I have no customers, only you people eating my food! Not that I mind, of course."

The man hurriedly backpedaled when Asher turned on him.

"Give them whatever they expect from this." Asher tossed a leather bag on the bar that landed with a heavy clunk. The innkeeper didn't bother to hide his enthusiasm as he tore at the string with greedy fingers, opening the bag to reveal a mix of gold and silver coins. A small fortune.

"Asher," Mendar stared at the bag, unable to finish the question in his mind.

"As I said before I left, we kill evil people now." Ander's tone took on an extra edge. "It turns out that one area where evil people excel is acquiring money. Once they're dead, it makes no sense to let it sit there, wouldn't you agree?"

Neither Mendar or the innkeeper answered his question. Mendar was too stunned and the innkeeper was too busy sorting the coins by type and size.

"Open this inn. An inn staying closed for this long makes no sense. We draw attention to ourselves for no reason. Throw a party or something, spend the money, draw a crowd. I want this business back to normal by tonight."

"Tonight?" the innkeeper spluttered. "But I..."

Once again, the man found himself swallowing his arguments when Asher turned his black eyes on him.

"What are you claiming? That you lack the intelligence, or that you lack the means? I just handed you the means, so all that remains is intelligence. How hard will you try to convince me that my faith is misplaced?"

The innkeeper froze for a moment, though somehow his hands continued to sort the coins, as if they acted on their own. Then, he smiled.

"I do hope to see you tonight at our grand re-opening, good sirs."

"Mendar, perhaps. Don't expect me. As the primary patron of your establishment, I expect you to keep the riff-raff out."

The innkeeper smiled, then the smile froze as he realized that Asher was referring to himself. He looked to Mendar for help, but he had none to give.

"Are you saying I should kick you out?" The innkeeper's voice quavered slightly at the very idea.

"If I ever come through that front door, I expect you to throw me out, yes. Try throwing something."

The innkeeper paled, but nodded his obedience.

"However, I shall require a new door or two installed on the side and back, something discreet. Maybe Mendar could be of some assistance."

At this point, Mendar felt dizzy. Was Asher now asking him for carpentry work? In all their years

164

together, he had never mentioned it even once.

Still, there was a kind of resolve entering the room. Even as changed as he was, Asher was back, he was giving orders and he had a plan. Even without knowing the plan or how crazy it was, that still made Mendar feel better.

There was something about this new Asher. He no longer swaggered, he stalked. He no longer lounged, he crouched, tight as a spring. He was closer now to the warrior Mendar had known during the war, but with a new edge to him.

It was deeply unsettling to see what had happened to his captain, but for the first time after a long stretch of doubt, he was starting to feel confident about their ability to take down the Tribulus.

All that remained was to see what price it would take.

Chapter 29

"People never look at trash."

Asher finally understood.

He had assumed it referred to her strategy of appearing like a homeless wreck so that she could move around without notice. And while that certainly happened, Asher now realized that there was a second portion of the saying, one she left unsaid: "But you should."

Just as Ander had checked with the tallow merchants to know when caravans were getting ready to leave, Baba looked at people's trash to know everything else.

Trash told you what people were trying to hide. Trash would tell you that the man who strutted about fine clothes was barely scraping by on beans and rice. Empty bottles and jugs would tell you who drank to excess. Every medical problem known to man created its own unique mix of refuse.

Trash told the truth.

All that week, as Baba mentored Asher in the art of secrets, they searched trash heaps. They visited garbage haulers who Baba paid to keep her informed of changes in patterns. Asher soon discovered that Baba commanded an information network that spanned the entire city.

A time of two, they were approached by wealthy men, who wore deep cloaks, spoke with respect, and thanked Baba for her discretion with a clink of gold coins in her hand.

In a couple instances, Asher intervened when they stumbled upon something truly wicked. Baba had stared at him in horror and fascination the first time he used his climbing hooks to kill a man.

Impressively, it was Asher who first noticed the discrepancy, not Baba.

"It was too much," he muttered.

She turned back to look at him.

"What was too much?"

"The tannery. There was too much trash. The wrong kinds. Too much food."

"I checked on that," she waved it away. "They feed their workers lunch every day, hence the food scraps. Apparently, it's really hard to keep workers at a tannery, the smell is too awful. But feeding them apparently works, they don't lose any employees."

Asher shook his head.

"Count the sacks. Each of those sacks carries twenty pounds of dried rice. Even if they only called the trash hauler once a week, that many empty bags would feed multiples of the number of workers we saw."

Baba looked back the way they had come.

"I can't believe I missed that," she muttered.

The two circled back to the tannery. Asher gathered an empty bottle on his way and clung to it as he "passed out" against a building across the street from the tannery. He didn't see where Baba chose her spot, but he heard her cursing at birds. The woman had a gift for appearing crazy. They'd overlook Asher, just one more drunken bum, but they'd actively avoid Baba. That would let her get closer.

The smell really was tremendous. Tanneries were famous for the pervasive odor. Asher didn't know much about the tanning process, but most outhouses smelled better. Why didn't finished leather reek?

He only had to wait, drooling against the building, before a bell rang, calling the workers to lunch. Most of them left the building to eat out in the slightly fresher air. Asher noted steaming plates of sliced beef, boiled corn, and hunks of hard bread.

No rice.

Baba had taught him that there was a certain power to being bored. It was one more kind of discomfort that could make a person stronger. Sitting there, slumped against the wall, Asher couldn't even move his head to look somewhere else, for fear of calling attention to himself, so he could only stare through half-closed eyes as the men worked their way through their meal. Asher let his mind be bored,

168

he could feel it rage for new stimulation, but Asher kept his eyes on the tannery and let his mind chew on the image like a dog with a bone.

No women.

While certain professions attracted more of one gender than another, Asher knew of no industry that didn't at least have a small mix.

There was not a single woman here. In fact, now that Asher had the idea in his head, he saw more. Not only were there no women, there were also no old men or boys. Every man there was in fighting trim. Asher might have expected such a trend from dock workers, but tanning had more to it than heavy lifting. There should have been some variety.

Then Baba was in amongst the men, begging for a morsel from their meals. One man tossed a half eaten corn cob into the dirt and Baba leapt at it, gnawing at the thing. The man laughed and others jumped in, throwing trash from their plate on top of the woman.

Baba cringed under the onslaught, which included some ceramic plates that hit hard. Then, she was choking. Most of the men backed away, but a couple edged closer, curious.

One got too close and Baba suddenly hacked up whatever had been caught in her throat. A sodden mess sprayed out of her mouth and splattered across the front of the man closest to her.

He stood, his arms out, for a full second of horror

before he kicked out, knocking Baba over.

"Get out of here!" he yelled, aiming another kick at her retreating backside as she skittered away.

Once she was gone, he inspected the filth on his shirt. He looked like he was going to be sick. Being careful to only touch the edges far from the muck stains, he lifted the shirt off.

A muscled arm flexed as he tossed the shirt away. Then he turned to look again where Baba had disappeared, turning his back to Asher across the street.

There, on this shoulder, was a perfectly straight white scar.

Chapter 30

"We've found them," Asher reported to Mendar back at the inn.

"Are you sure it's not one of the regional centers? The only real advantage we have right now is that they think you're dead. As soon as we hit anything of theirs, the whole anthill is going up. You'd better be certain."

"We watched until nightfall. Even after the regular workers left, the place still had a heavy guard all through the night. Far more than a tannery would require."

Mendar hemmed.

"I don't know, that seems pretty thin."

A now rare smile tugged at Asher's mouth.

"I know, that's why I stayed until morning and saw Raca enter the building."

Mendar was not amused.

"You fed me this whole story about rice and guards? You could have just said, 'I saw Raca.'"

"But then you wouldn't know how clever I was finding the place," Asher shot back.

Mendar reached for his daggers and sword and

started strapping them on. He didn't have to ask what happened next. Once Asher had direction, he added momentum. Now, they would attack.

"Where are you going?" Asher asked him.

"I'm going with you to that tannery." Mendar settled the belt on his hips and pulled his sword from its sheath, doing a quick check over the blade. "I am going to kick down the doors, and I am going to slaughter a room full of child-grabbing Tribulus scum."

Asher shook his head.

"Right now, I'm going by myself."

"No chance!" Mendar spat the words like a curse. He had already been feeling left out as Asher and Baba investigated around the city. "You brought me here for killing, Captain. You're good at it, I'm good at it, and together we're a meat grinder. Don't you push me to the side now. Don't you dare!"

Asher stood and faced his lieutenant, taking in his red face and the vein pulsing in his neck.

"In the beginning, I might have brought you here for killing, but that's not why you're here now."

Asher reached out and pulled Mendar into an embrace.

"You are here because you are my friend."

Then he pulled back. Even this new Asher wasn't much of a hugger. Still, there had to be a first time for everything.

"Right now, I need you for something better than

rampaging. Besides, I don't think kicking down the door is going to work this time. It's a very solid door, and these are trained fighters at the core of their operation."

Then, Asher sat down with his friend and explained his plan.

"Can you do that?" Asher asked after he was finished.

Mendar grinned widely.

"Oh, Captain, I can do that."

Chapter 31

Tannery wagons stank of chemicals and rotting meat. This one also reeked of excrement. The wagons were parked outside of the building. It hadn't been difficult to figure out that one of the wagons was being used to sneak out the waste of the prisoners. So, Asher found himself a hole, buried down amidst the barrels and waited until morning, when the wagon would do its run.

Asher counted on the hideous smell to keep anyone from checking this wagon very thoroughly before they hitched it up and drove it into the loading bay of the tannery. Two men grabbed empty barrels and carried them toward the back of the building.

Asher rolled out of the wagon and slipped under a nearby table. He took a moment to breathe, but kept his eye on the two men and their barrels. One paused to take off a lock from a pair of heavy doors set into the floor.

Asher smiled.

The workers pulled the doors open and carried their barrels down under ground.

It was common for tanneries to keep tanks

underground for drainage from the large tanning vats above. It wouldn't have been hard to carve out some extra space under there to form workable dungeons. Asher watched and waited for his moment.

As usual, Baba didn't keep him waiting long. He'd only hidden under the table for a few minutes when the call came.

"Fire!"

It was only one of the wagons outside, but the danger of it spreading and the sheer spectacle drew every man to that side of the tannery. Asher slipped out and strode quickly across the floor, finding the large doors and the lock that held it closed.

It was a small lock, and made of cheap iron, one good blow with a sword would break it. After all, it was being used to keep in children, not cattle.

So Asher drew out a much larger lock, one used for gates in the feedlots. The hasp was thick steel, meant to hold a gate closed against a bull. He reached down and threaded a matching chain through the handles of the doors and secured the chain with his massive lock.

There.

The children had been the one great flaw in Mendar's "slaughter everyone" plan. After all, the children were being kept here as hostages. How much of an attack would it take before somebody thought to start using those hostages?

They had been in danger, trapped there under

Raca's lock and key. Now they were safe and sound, under Asher's lock and key.

He turned back towards the main door and started walking.

"Hey! Who is that!" A voice called down from the inspection floor above. Asher turned to look.

It was Raca.

His eyes narrowed for a moment as he tried to place this black shape creeping through his tannery floor. Then his eyes shot wide and his voice roared.

"It's Asher! Everyone! Get him!"

Raca went from calm, to amazed, to apoplectic in two short heartbeats. He pulled his own sword and started running toward the stairs. Asher turned and continued his path to the main gate. Dozens of men had now turned, first to look at Raca, as he continued to scramble and point, then they looked to where he was pointing.

Steel sang as swords and daggers leapt from sheaths and the men surged forward.

They were twenty yards away as Asher lifted the beam holding the main gate closed.

They were ten yards away when he tugged at the giant, broad doors.

And they were five yards away when Mendar pushed through the doors from the other side, followed by two dozen proven killers of men.

Chapter 32

Asher's death squad from the war, scarred and hard, came through the door and went about the work they knew best.

Raca's men had been trained in the same way, of course, but there was something Raca had missed. He had asked what could be proved by standing still during a beating, by keeping quiet while cut. The answer became obvious as the genuine article met the counterfeits:

Discipline.

When one of Raca's men got cut, they would wince and stumble. When one of Asher's men got cut, they would cut back.

When one of Raca's men got cornered, they would surrender. When one of Asher's men got cornered, they would settle into a stance and see how many of the enemy they could take with them.

Raca's men hacked and slashed with anger, hatred, and, in the end, fear. Asher's men killed with aggression and efficiency. The mob met the machine.

Asher dropped his hooks from his sleeves and circled wide around the main fight. Sure enough, three men had already retreated back to the wide doors set in the floor. Having discovered Asher's lock barring their way, one of them had grabbed an axe and was hammering away at the chain.

The two anxious men beside him saw Asher coming and sounded the alarm. The man with the axe turned and swung at Asher. He twisted easily out of the way, using his speed to counter the other man's strength. He reached out a hook and with a quick jerk snagged the man's arm at the bicep, just above the elbow.

The man roared in pain, though he managed to keep hold of the axe with one hand. That didn't save him, though, as Asher continued past the man, bringing his arm along with him and spinning the man as he tried to free his arm or bring the heavy axe into play with one hand. Asher dragged the man forward a couple steps, which placed the big man between Asher and his two friends.

Asher took advantage of the opening and brought his other hook up and snagged it on the man's shoulder, up by the neck. The man roared like a bull, but the sound cut off abruptly as Asher used the anchor point to drag the man down as he jumped up, connecting his knee with the man's chin. The man's head rocked back and then forward again as he fell to the floor. The hooks ripped loose, leaving jagged wounds.

Asher settled back into his stance, the hooks, now

bloody, hanging low. The two other men paused, looking between Asher and the brutal melee behind them.

Then they were running to the side door, trying to escape. Asher ran them down in three paces, reaching down to snag at their running legs with his hooks. The end came quickly after that.

Asher looked out at the killing floor, where his men were mopping up the last of the Tribulus.

Many of them looked at him expectantly. It took a moment for him to realize what they were waiting for.

They were waiting for him to laugh. But as Asher looked around the bloody tannery, he didn't feel like laughing. Something had changed. These hadn't been hardened warriors, like the Marauders. They had been thugs and criminals. Asher and his men hadn't won a battle. They had exterminated vermin.

They had gathered the prisoners in the center, watched over by five guards, Mendar among them.

Asher walked over to greet Mendar.

"What do you want us to do with the prisoners?" Mendar asked. Asher looked them over, surprised to find Raca among them. The man looked up and scowled at Asher.

"How about that duel now, Captain?" Raca challenged. "Make your men promise to let me leave if I win. Let's end this now between us. What say you?"

Asher turned back to Mendar.

"These are all bad men, lieutenant."

Mendar nodded, understanding. He turned to the other men he had guarding them.

"Kill them all."

The screams only lasted seconds.

Chapter 33

King Stephan woke to darkness. He didn't know why he had woken up. He rolled over slightly to glance at his wife, sleeping next to him in the bed. As he rolled, his leg met a familiar lump and he looked down to find Tibian, who had crawled into bed down by his legs. Stephan rolled his eyes. Probably another nightmare. The boy was prone to them.

Stephan looked back at his pillow, but sleep had fled. The night felt wrong. He reached behind the bedpost, where he kept a dagger hidden. Its weight often comforted him. It wasn't there.

Stephan's sense of unease grew sharper. He swung his feet over the side of the bed. He reached for his slippers. They weren't there either. He scowled.

There was an oil lamp on a stone table by his bed. It was kept lit, but hooded during the night. With a cautious glance backwards at his wife, he reached out to raise the hood ever so slightly.

"Actually, I prefer the dark."

Stephan froze. The voice was quiet and close, incredibly close. His mind raced. If this were an assassin, it was already too late. Was there a way to save his wife and son?

"I'm not here to kill you, my most illustrious liege." The whisper in the night mocked him, even as it seemed to read his mind.

"Then why are you here?" Stephan whispered back. "What audacity is this? Who are you?"

"Hunger."

A chill ran through Stephan. He had heard that Eliana had died. As soon as he heard it, he had ordered the castle guards doubled. He had no idea how Asher would react to having his one tie to humanity suddenly cut.

"Did you kill my guards?" Stephan hissed, hoping he hadn't slept through a massacre.

"As far as I know, they are still diligently prowling the halls. I have no need to hurt them, they weren't in my way."

"Why are you here?"

"We need to talk. Here." Two lumps landed in Stephan's lap. His slippers. "Put these on and follow me."

Stephan did as instructed, happy to create a little distance between Asher and his sleeping family. Maybe if he could create a distraction, he could signal the guards.

Unfortunately, they only went as far as the small anteroom, which his wife had been using as a closet. Once they were both in and out of line of sight of the bed, Asher raised the hood of the oil lamp he'd been carrying. In spite of himself, Stephan gasped.

This was not the same man who had knelt before him a mere three weeks earlier. The beautiful black hair was gone, hacked away. Asher's fine features were drawn, wrinkles at the corners of his eyes. The man looked like a stray dog.

Stephan's eyes flicked down to his waist, and was surprised to see the sword missing.

He drew no comfort from the fact. Rabid dogs didn't carry swords, either, but that didn't make them any less dangerous.

"The leader of the Tribulus is dead. The children they kidnapped are being returned to their families. They are a little worse for wear, but they'll survive."

Stephan let out a breath he hadn't realized he was holding.

"Thank you, Asher!" He felt a great weight lift from his shoulders. "The rumors were true, then? Our nation owes you a debt."

"I'm glad to hear you say that, my king."

Stephan tensed again. He had been distracted by his relief and had forgotten for one blissful second that he stood within arm's reach of the Laughing Killer.

"What do you want? I can still release the statement saying you're a hero."

The dim, flickering light played shadows over Asher's face as he sneered.

"I no longer have any need for such publicity. In fact, what I want from you will take even less effort."

"Oh?"

"Keep your mouth shut and one eye closed."

Stephan set his jaw. Even in his nightclothes, he was still king. This wouldn't stand.

"No one is outside the law, Asher. I'm not trading the horrors of the Tribulus for your own criminal empire. No deal."

"You're a brave man, my king." While he knew the comment must be sarcastic, Stephan somehow couldn't hear the flippancy in Asher's voice. He had sounded sincere. "But you are also wrong. I have spent these last weeks among people who are outside your law, outside your reach, and outside your protection."

Stephan knew what he was talking about, but refused to give ground.

"That is only temporary," he insisted. "As we recruit and train more guards, we will be able to police more and more of the kingdom. Just because we can't enforce it perfectly doesn't mean we should abandon the law."

"You know, I believe that you will try. I'll even make you a deal. When your guards can take over and keep the smelliest corner of your kingdom safe, I'll step aside. Until then, I will dispose of evil in any way I see fit."

Stephan blinked for a moment as he realized what

184

Asher had been suggesting. He had assumed that Asher had been taunting him, claiming that Stephan wouldn't be able to catch or punish him. He shook his head.

"No, no, no. I told you before, I'm not looking for a royal assassin."

Asher reached out and grabbed his chin, pulling him close, Asher's jet black eyes boring into his.

"That is a crying shame, my king, because you've got one. I meant what I said. If the day comes that you can bring your courts and guards into the slums, I'll walk away. In the meantime, my men and I will make evil men disappear. Don't come after us and we won't come after you."

Asher released him and re-hooded the lamp, darkness washing back over the anteroom.

"Enjoy your night's rest." Asher's voice retreated through the darkness. Stephan came out of the anteroom in time to see Asher, a vague shape in the scattered moonlight from the window. He paused by the bed and looked down at the sleeping Tibian.

"I envy you your son," he whispered, too low for Stephan to hear across the room.

Then the hooks were out of his sleeves and he was out of the window. Stephan considered shouting for the guards, then stopped and considered.

It wasn't right. He knew that in his very soul. Bad people killing other bad people wasn't justice. It wasn't law. He walked over to the bed and sat down, sinking his head into his hands. His people deserved better, he knew that.

King Stephan sighed.

He also knew that he couldn't give it to them, at least not yet. Being a king didn't make him a god, and there were severe limits on his power. He couldn't stop the sinking feeling in the pit of his stomach as he thought about Asher out there, murdering on the streets, guided only by his own dubious conscience.

Right then and there, Stephan decided that he would arrest Asher and make him stand trial for his crimes, as soon as he had the men and resources to make it happen. But for tonight...

King Stephan kicked off his slippers and lifted his feet up into the bed, careful of little Tibian. Then he laid his head on his pillow and went back to sleep.

Author's Note

In a world where love has many counterfeits, I've seen people glorify the wrong kind of relationships. Joker and Harley Quinn come immediately to mind. I recognize that there is a possibility in my own work of people seeing Asher and Eliana as some great love story.

Let me be clear, they are not.

Specifically, we can look at Asher's behavior of keeping her isolated, and thinking of their relationship primarily in terms of possession and what he gets out of it. This is toxic behavior.

At the end of the day, Asher is a sociopath, as evidenced by his lack of empathy and extreme difficulty in forming real relationships, even with the men he trained and fought with. His relationship with Eliana is not a healthy one.

Obsession is not love.

Possession is not devotion.

Accept no counterfeit love, my friends.

About the Author

Lance Conrad lives in Utah, surrounded by loving and supportive family who are endlessly patient with his many eccentricities. His passion for writing comes from the belief that there are great lessons to be learned as we struggle with our favorite characters in fiction. He spends his time reading, writing, building lasers, and searching out new additions to his impressive collection of gourmet vinegars.

Find out more about Lance and his books on his website:
www.lanceconradbooks.com

To support the author, consider leaving a review on Amazon

www.ingramcontent.com/pod-product-compliance
Lightning Source LLC
Chambersburg PA
CBHW071513170626
46811CB00007B/2837